Classics of Modern Science Fiction

THE SHORES OF ANOTHER SEA

Volume 3

Books by Chad Oliver

NOVELS
Mists of Dawn (1952)
Shadows in the Sun (1954)
The Winds of Time (1957)
Unearthly Neighbors (1960)
The Wolf Is My Brother (1967)

STORIES
Another Kind (1955)
The Edge of Forever (1971)

NONFICTION
Cultural Anthropology:
The Discovery of Humanity (1980)

Classics of Modern Science Fiction

THE SHORES OF ANOTHER SEA

CHAD OLIVER

Volume 3

Introduction by George Zebrowski
Foreword by Isaac Asimov

Series Editor: George Zebrowski

CROWN PUBLISHERS, INC.
NEW YORK

To
Bob Edgerton
and
Bud Winans

Copyright © 1971 by Chad Oliver
All rights reserved. No part of this book may be reproduced or
transmitted in any form or by any means, electronic or
mechanical, including photocopying, recording, or by any
information storage and retrieval system, without permission in
writing from the publisher.
Published by Crown Publishers, Inc., One Park Avenue, New
York, New York 10016 and simultaneously in Canada by
General Publishing Company Limited
Manufactured in the United States of America
Library of Congress Cataloging in Publication Data
Oliver, Chad, 1928–
The shores of another sea.
(Classics of modern science fiction; v. 3)
Reprint. Originally published: London: Gollancz, 1971.
I. Title. II. Series.
PS3565.L458S5 1984 813'.54 83-23214
ISBN 0-517-55186-1
Book design by Lauren Dong
First Crown Edition 1984

Retrieving the Lost
by Isaac Asimov

The history of contemporary science fiction begins with the spring of 1926, when the first magazine ever to be devoted entirely to science fiction made its appearance. For a quarter-century thereafter science fiction continued to appear in magazines—and only in magazines.

They were wonderful days for those of us who lived through them, but there was a flaw. Magazines are, by their very nature, ephemeral. They are on the newsstands a month or two and are gone. A very few readers may save their issues, but they are fragile and do not stand much handling.

Beginning in 1950, science fiction in book form began to make its appearance, and some of the books retrieved the magazine short stories and serials in the form of collections, anthologies and novels. As time went on, however, it became clear that the vast majority of science-fiction books were in paperback form, and these, too, were ephemeral. Their stay on the newsstands is not entirely calendar-bound, and they can withstand a bit more handling than periodicals can—but paperbacks tend to be, like magazines, throwaway items.

That leaves the hardback book, which finds its way into public libraries as well as private homes, and which is durable. Even there, we have deficiencies. The relatively few science-fiction books which appear in hardback usually appear in small printings and few, if any, reprintings. Out-of-print is the usual fate, and often a not very long delayed one, at that.

Some science-fiction books have endured, remaining available in hardcover form for years, even decades, and appearing in repeated paperback reincarnations. We all know which these are because, by enduring, they have come to be read by millions, including you and me.

It is, of course, easy to argue that the test of time and popularity has succeeded in separating the gold from the dross, and that we have with us all the science-fiction books that have deserved to endure.

That, however, is too easy a dismissal. It is an interesting and convenient theory, but the world of human affairs is far too complex to fit into theories, especially convenient ones. It sometimes takes time to recognize quality, and the time required is sometimes longer than the visible existence of a particular book. That the quality of a book is not recognizable at once need not be a sign of deficiency, but rather a sign of subtlety. It is not being particularly paradoxical to point out that a book may be, in some cases, too good to be immediately popular. And then, thanks to the mechanics of literary ephemerality, realization of the fact may come too late.

Or must it?

Suppose there are dedicated and thoughtful writers and scholars like George Zebrowski and Martin H. Greenberg, who have been reading science fiction intensively, and with educated taste, for decades. And suppose there is a publisher such as Crown Publishers, Inc. which is interested in providing a second chance for quality science fiction which was undervalued the first time around.

In that case we end up with Crown's *Classics of Modern Science Fiction* in which the lost is retrieved, the unjustly forgotten is remembered, and the undervalued is resurrected. And you are holding a sample in your hand.

Naturally, the revival of these classics will benefit the publisher, the editors, and the writers, but that is almost by the way. The real beneficiaries will be the readers, among whom the older are likely to taste again delicacies they had all but forgotten, while the younger will encounter delights of whose existence they were unaware.

Read—

And enjoy.

Introduction
by George Zebrowski

Kingsley Amis, writing about Chad Oliver's second published novel, *Shadows In The Sun*, seems to have thought that a six-foot, two hundred pound American anthropologist from Texas, dressed in a wide-brimmed hat, khaki shirt and trousers, Ph.D. well hidden, was an unlikely hero for a science-fiction story; yet this was nothing more than a fair description of Chad Oliver himself. From one picture I've seen, Chad Oliver could easily pass for John D. MacDonald's popular sleuth, the thoughtful yet adventurous Travis McGee. Amis's lapse into parochialism was laughable in a critic who professed to being a reader of science fiction, especially when he was discussing a novel about a first encounter with an alien civilization.

The first book I read by Chad Oliver was *Mists of Dawn*, a young-adult novel published in 1952 as part of a distinguished science-fiction program presented by

Winston. These books set a standard for young-adult science fiction which, together with the books published by Robert A. Heinlein and Andre Norton, has rarely been bettered. *Mists of Dawn*, which I came upon in 1958, was also one of the first science-fiction novels I read. I remember being struck by the sympathetic account of the early humans depicted in the story; and the time-travel adventure enthralled me so completely that I read the book at one sitting. Chad Oliver became one of my favorite writers. And there were even better books to come by the same author!

Chad Oliver belongs to that distinguished group of science-fiction writers who are also scientists. The list includes Isaac Asimov, Gregory Benford, and Arthur C. Clarke, among others; but Oliver is the only anthropologist in this group, and as such he has brought a deep sense of humanity into his writing. It was the qualities of compassion, attention to mood and thoughtfulness and character, together with a constant awareness of a larger horizon to human history—looking back in time as well as forward into the future—that kept me reading Oliver's work.

When his first story collection, *Another Kind* (1955) appeared, Damon Knight immediately noticed that Oliver was "building up our field's most fascinating and comprehensive collection of anthropological science fiction." Anthony Boucher praised *Another Kind* as the "outstanding science-fiction book of the year." And this was only the author's third book (*Mists of Dawn* was followed by *Shadows in The Sun* in 1954). A comparable working of an-

thropological themes was not to be seen until the
appearance of Ursula K. Le Guin and Michael Bishop in
the 1960s and 1970s.

The Shores of Another Sea, Oliver's sixth novel, was
published as a paperback original in 1971, and as a British
hardcover in the same year; it received excellent notices in
England. It followed *The Wolf Is My Brother* (1967), which
won the Spur Award as best western historical novel of the
year, given by the Western Writers of America. Oliver had
every reason to feel encouraged, but the American paperback of *Shores* was neglected. It was not reviewed in any of
the science-fiction magazines, not even in *Analog*, where
Oliver was well known. One suspects that the printing was
small and that few review copies were sent out.

Shores is set in Kenya, where Oliver spent some time
doing anthropological research. It's a novel in which personal experience is perfectly blended with the science-
fictional theme of first contact. Dean McLaughlin has
called the novel "the most marvelously understated first
contact story I have ever found. So quietly real you know it
could have happened. Maybe it did."

As the novel unfolds, an unnerving analogy begins to
emerge: we are to the baboons of the story as the alien
visitors are to us. A subtle guilt begins to operate on the
reader, recalling not only the horrors of the white man's
treatment of Africa but also our treatment of the planet's
animal life. Only Arthur C. Clarke, in *The Deep Range*,
has given our treatment of Earth's animals something of
the pointed consideration which the problem gets in
Oliver's novel. It is a work rich in resonances and ironies,

and Kenya's colonial past makes the reader tremble as the characters are overtaken by the full development of the central situation. It would be unfair of me to reveal more of the story in an introduction; but I will say that the stresses and strains of the story, together with its deeply felt emotional core, will involve the reader completely. I read this one in one sitting also. Hemingway could not have written a better book.

The best and brightest of science fiction's critics and reviewers responded well to Oliver's two decades of science fiction. Anthony Boucher placed him in the front rank with Heinlein, Clarke, and Asimov. More recently, Gary K. Wolfe, writing in *Twentieth Century Science Fiction Writers* (St. Martin's, 1981), has said that Oliver's "real strengths lie in the construction of hypothetical anthropological problems and his graceful, understated style. *Unearthly Neighbors* (1960) may be the most carefully reasoned account of the problems of making contact with an alien culture in all science fiction." Wolfe also credits Oliver as being solely responsible for introducing well-thought-out anthropological themes into science fiction. His work is "valuable both for the specific insights it offers and for the importance it holds in the developing sophistication of the genre." Damon Knight summed up Oliver's talent best: "Oliver has the kind of gift this field sorely lacks—the ability to touch the heart of the human problem."

One error about Oliver's writing career deserves to be cleared up: he has not stopped writing fiction. Contrary to one mistake-filled reference work, his last novel was published in 1976, not 1971. Short fiction has continued to appear throughout the last decade in such anthologies as *Again, Dangerous Visions*, in the *Continuum* series, and in *Future Quest* and *Future Kin*. In 1981, new stories were published in *Analog* and in Fred Saberhagen's *A Spadeful of Spacetime*. Another story, "Ghost Town," appeared in *Analog* in 1983. A work of nonfiction, *The Discovery of Humanity: An Introduction to Anthropology* was published in 1981. From my conversations with the author, I have every reason to believe that this new edition of *Shores* signals a new burst of novel-length works to come.

And if by chance you make a landfall on the shores of another sea in a far country inhabited by savages and barbarians, remember you this: the greatest danger and the surest hope lies not with fires and arrows but in the quicksilver hearts of men.

—ADVICE TO NAVIGATORS (1744)

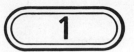

1

I T BEGAN AS a perfectly ordinary day—ordinary, that is,
for the Baboonery.

Royce Crawford frowned at his crippled typewriter.
He filled his pipe with tobacco from a yellow Sweet Nut
tin, and lit it. It wasn't the best tobacco in the world, but it
had one decisive advantage over all other brands: it was the
only kind he could get. He could buy Sweet Nut for a few
bob anywhere in Kenya, even at the *duka* in Mitaboni, and
that made it extra special. He puffed on the pipe and
stared at the bare plank walls of the little room he used as
an office. The door was open and he could see into the
main operating room across the hall. The clean white
table was empty. The clamps were relaxed and waiting.
They had been waiting for a long time now.

He had to finish his monthly report to Wallace, which
was a chore he detested at the best of times. And this,
emphatically, was not the best of times. Royce knew that
something was wrong, but he had no solid facts at his

disposal. He had an impression, a crawling sensation on his back, a feeling of unease. For three days he had felt that he was being . . . watched.

Royce was not an unduly fanciful man. He was singularly unworried by dreams. He wouldn't have known an omen if he tripped over one. In his scheme of things, premonitions were in a class with astrology and female vapors. At the same time, he was not a clod with a muscle for a brain. Royce had led an unusual life and he was no stranger to trouble. He had learned to trust himself when he could not rely on others. When he had a hunch it generally meant something. As far as he was concerned, if he felt that he was being watched it meant just that.

Something had him under observation.

A man cannot be a hunter without knowing what it is to be hunted.

He couldn't tell that to Wallace, of course. Wallace was a long way from the Baboonery. He was in another world.

Royce shifted in his chair and looked out the window. The window was open, as always, for the excellent reason that it could not be shut. It had a screen in it, but no glass. This alone marked the Baboonery as an American enterprise: most of the British-built structures in Kenya had glass windows and no screens. On the whole, he supposed, the system worked pretty well. The majority of the British houses—some still British, some not—were in the highlands where the weather was often chilly. It never got cold at the Baboonery.

Maybe that was part of the trouble, he thought without conviction. The weather *was* getting on his nerves. It was dry, bone dry, and it was hot. There was nothing green as far as the eye could see. The red dust was everywhere, like a crust of rusted iron. Even the elephants were a light reddish color, pink elephants for real; they would not be gray again until the short rains came. The baboons sat in their rows of cages and peered out along their snouts at a world that seemed too barren to support life. The parched dry banana leaves rustled in the steady arid wind like a mockery of rain. From somewhere around the main building, out of his line of vision, he could hear the tuneless song of Mbali, the shamba boy. It was a curious song: haunting but formless, it faded on the wind and could never be quite recalled when the singer stopped.

Royce's pipe went out and he lit it again. He pulled up the typewriter. Ben Wallace knew what the Baboonery was like. He had spent a lot of time there. He knew all about the heat and the politics and the men who could suddenly turn alien just when you thought you had them figured out. Royce thought of Wallace on the other end of the report he had to write, Wallace sitting there at his compulsively neat desk at the Foundation office in Houston. It was late September. The air conditioning would still be going full blast in Houston. There would be mobs at the Astrodome, watching the Astros limp valiantly through another season. Ben Wallace would be dressed in one of his sincere dark suits—wrinkle-free, lint-free, bulge-free. Wallace would want some facts, not impressions.

Okay. Royce typed the familiar heading: Kikumbuliu Primate Research Station, P.O. Mitaboni, Kenya, East

Africa. He supplied the date and proceeded to confine himself to essentials. He had forty baboons on hand, fifteen of them female. He would ship twenty animals to Houston within three weeks, sending them by train to Nairobi and then putting them on the plane himself at Embakasi. The other twenty baboons were still undergoing tests of various sorts; he included information on the condition of each animal. The only unusual expenses—and they were becoming something less than unusual—involved repairs to the starter on the Land Rover and to the generator for the Baboonery electrical system. He added that he, his wife, and the two kids were all well, signed the report, and that was that.

Royce Crawford stood up, stretched, and glanced at his watch. It was after two. He would have to shake a leg. The men needed meat and he might have to go all the way to the Tsavo to get it. It had to be today; Donaldson would be coming in within the next day or two, and Donaldson did not take kindly to hunting when he was wet-nursing a safari.

Royce grabbed an evelope—already stamped and addressed to the Foundation—and walked out into the African sunlight.

It took Royce a good hour to do what he had to do. He sent the battered lorry into Mitaboni twenty-five miles away to air-mail the report and pick up some supplies. He checked the baboon cages to make certain they were clean and secure. He took his .375 out of the gun safe in the breezeway between the kitchen and his bedroom. He helped Kathy get the children down for their afternoon nap. He drank a cup of ferocious coffee.

Then he was as free as a man can be, and despite his nagging worry he was content. It was good to have a task ahead of him that was pure pleasure. There weren't many jobs like that left in the world.

The Land Rover, miraculously, started on the first try. It was a wide-wheel-base model with a tarp that stretched over a frame in back of the cab. In the dry seasons, the tarp wasn't used; the Land Rover, in effect, became a pick-up truck not unlike the ones Royce had used back in Texas. When he hunted, Royce rode in back with Mutisya. Kilatya, God help him, did the driving.

There were three dirt roads, little more than trails, that led away from the cluster of buildings that was the Baboonery. One, straight as a drunken snake, went ten miles through the bush to join the main road that connected Mombasa on the Indian Ocean with Nairobi in the heart of Kenya. A second road more or less followed the railway, crossed the Tsavo River, and ultimately—if you were lucky—led into Mitaboni. It was shorter than going to Mitaboni by way of the main road, but it was so rough that it took twice the travel time. The third road, impossible for anything except a vehicle equipped with four-wheel drive, went straight into the bush. It was strictly a hunter's trail; it did not lead to anything except a bluff overlooking the Tsavo River. To Royce, it was the most pleasant road in the world. There was something to be said, after all, for the old roads—the winding country lanes, the gravel farm roads he had known at home, the packed brown ruts that led to pastures and barns and weathered frame houses. It was a loss that all the roads back home had turned to ribbons of cement. A man could move in a hurry on those roads, but there was nowhere worth going.

They took the third road.

Royce balanced easily in the back of the Land Rover, one hand holding the .375 and the other resting on the metal frame. His wide-brimmed Texas hat shielded his eyes from the sun and the jolting vehicle could not go fast enough on that road to make the wind a problem. He felt no compulsion to speak, and neither did Mutisya. They knew their jobs.

For a moment, it was not very different from setting out on a whitetail hunt back home. Royce had ridden in a thousand pick-ups on a thousand days like this one: hat clamped on his head, the feel of the rifle in his hand, the always-new sense of peace and expectancy in his heart.

In less than a minute the Baboonery was invisible behind them, screened by the bush and a slight dip in the land. It was an astonishing transition; Royce never got used to it. Within a few hundred yards he was in another world, an older world, and—perhaps—a better world.

He knew that he could never describe it to anyone, not really. He had tried, in some of the hunting articles he had written, but he had never come close. It had to be experienced. It had to be seen and smelled and heard. A man had to bring something of himself to it. Some men, the dead ones that still walked, never could feel it. They were the men who might glance at a trout stream in the Rockies and see just another creek.

There was the sky, that immense African sky that was

like no other sky on earth. There was the land, now choked with thickets of thorny brush, now opening up into great meadows dotted with graceful flat-topped acacias and grotesque swollen-trunked baobabs. There were the colors, subdued now after the drought: long tawny grass the color of lions, red dust that powdered the earth, the dead gray-green of what was left of the vegetation. There were the birds, countless birds, birds on the ground and in the trees and darting through the clean air. Most of all, there was a feeling that time had no meaning here; time was somehow suspended. It was an illusion, of course, but it was a good illusion.

The Land Rover pushed its way through a thick clump of brush. The tsetse flies came out in a cloud; they were always there, at that particular place, waiting. They settled on Royce and Mutisya, going for the patches of exposed skin. The devils hurt. It wasn't just a matter of worrying about the sickness the flies sometimes carried. They were long, tough flies, and they bit until they drew blood. It was impossible to brush them away. You had to pick them off your skin and kill them one by one. Flies, Royce thought, were the curse of Africa. Flies and ants. The pretty picture books always left them out, but they were ubiquitous. He had seen the ants so thick that bedposts had to be placed in cans of gasoline before a person could sleep in safety. He had seen tsetse flies go after a herd of skinny cattle and turn their hides into raw sores. He had seen common flies so numerous in African villages that children would sit with flies in their noses and ears and eyes and refuse to make the hopeless effort to chase them away.

Fortunately, the tsetse fly cannot live in open country.

As soon as the Land Rover emerged from the thick brush the flies were gone. Royce didn't expect to encounter them again until they passed through the same clump of brush on the way back to the Baboonery.

He felt a wonderful sense of freedom, as though he had just been released from prison. Royce had never been a city man when he could avoid it, and this was a world where the city was only a faded memory of thronging unhappy people and jangling noises and filth that had once been air. Life could be dangerous here but it was not complicated. A man would win or lose on his own personal ability. He was not just a puppet jerking on a string.

The Land Rover bumped to a stop as Kilatya engaged the low-ratio four-wheel drive. They went over the edge of the cut made by the Kikumbuliu River—little more than a trickle of water now—and splashed through the bed of the stream. The other bank was steep and it was hard to hang on as the Land Rover churned its way back up to level ground.

The land opened up before them in a vast level plain. The trail ran along in a reasonably straight line that roughly paralleled the Kikumbuliu on their right. On the far side of the river there was a rocky ridge. On the near side there was only a sweep of sun-drenched miles that led away to the Tsavo. There was a light breeze blowing and it was cool and comfortable.

Mutisya watched to the right and Royce to the left. There was nothing to it; the game was thick. In less than a minute Mutisya caught his arm and pointed. Royce caught a glimpse of gray with vertical white stripes. Kudu.

Royce knocked with his fist on the top of the cab. Kilatya, as usual, kept on going. Royce leaned forward and hollered into the open window. "*Simama!*" he said. "Stop!"

The Land Rover jerked to a quick halt as Kilatya hit the brakes, driving with his customary delicacy of touch. Royce was thrown forward almost over the cab. He grabbed his field glasses. It took him only a few seconds to pick the animals up. There were four or five kudu out there.

He considered trying a shot from the Land Rover, where he could use the top of the cab as a rest for his heavy rifle. But even as he watched the antelopes moved away from him, screening themselves with brush. They were a good two hundred yards away.

He jumped down to the ground. "*Haya!*" he said. "Come on!"

Mutisya did not need to be told what to do. He had hunted kudu when Royce's only knowledge of Africa had come from Tarzan books. Still, he smiled. He rather liked Royce, and he was used to redundant orders from white men.

They struck off through the bush, keeping downwind from the kudu and making use of what cover there was. They moved fast; it was not difficult country in the dry season, and there was no particular need for caution. Royce had a healthy respect for mambas and puff adders, but they were no more common in Africa than rattlesnakes were in Texas and it was absurd to go about in constant fear of them. As for the dangerous animals—lion, elephant, rhino, water buffalo—a reasonable prudence was all that was necessary.

He could not see the kudu but he knew where they were. They would not move very far unless they were seriously alarmed. They had a trick of running off for a short distance and then stopping. They would often stand quite still and look at a hunter until he fired.

Mutisya spotted them first. He crouched down behind a bush, saying nothing. Royce dropped to one knee. He could see three of them clearly. One ram had his head up, listening. He was not over one hundred yards away.

It was a piece of cake. Royce lifted the heavy .375 to his shoulder and peered through the scope. The kudu presented a natural target; Royce drew a bead just between the first two vertical white stripes. He squeezed the trigger. The big rifle bucked against his shoulder and the flat sound of the shot shattered the afternoon silence.

The kudu dropped with the startling suddenness of a man clubbed with an iron crowbar. They wouldn't have to track that one. The other animals ran off with the shot, bounding away with the white undersides of their tails showing curved up over their rumps.

Royce was shaking a little, but he was grinning from ear to ear. It had been a clean shot. The regret would come later. There was still something in a man that responded to a kill—something, perhaps, that dated from a time when there was no latitude for sentiment.

"*Mzuri*," Mutisya said quietly. "Good."

Royce sent Mutisya back to tell Kilatya to bring up the Land Rover. Then he walked over and looked at his kill.

The antelope was beautiful, even in death. The gray coat with the white stripes was dusty but sleek. The graceful horns were in good shape. It was a so-called lesser kudu, of course; Royce had never even seen the greater kudu. Nevertheless, it was quite an animal.

It had the soft, sad eyes of death.

The Land Rover pushed up through the brush like a tank. Royce opened the tail gate, and the three men wrestled the kudu into the back of the vehicle. It wasn't an easy job; the kudu was over two hundred pounds of dead weight. When they got him inside, Royce put up the tail gate again.

That was all there was to it.

Royce pulled out his pipe and lit it. He glanced at his watch. It was only four-thirty. A good two hours of daylight left.

Plenty of time. He did not want to go back to the Baboonery. He felt secure here, at ease. The feeling of being watched was somehow diminished. It was as though it was the Baboonery itself that was under observation, and when he moved away from it he moved outside a zone, like an animal stepping beyond the area swept by field glasses. . . .

If he went on, he might see Buck again.

He told Kilatya to push on to the Tsavo and climbed in next to the dead kudu. The flies were beginning to gather around the darkening blood on the animal's shoulder. He could smell the blood.

He felt better when the vehicle started and he could drink the cleansing wind.

The land was softer now, and more mysterious. Much of its naked harshness was gone. The shadows cast by the lowering sun broke up the stark outlines and created depths, as though a flat picture had suddenly become three-dimensional. The world was very still except for the whine of the Land Rover's engine.

The trail angled away from the Kikumbuliu and stretched out in an easy descent across the sloping plain that led to the Tsavo. There was not much brush here and Royce could see for miles. There were elephant droppings along the pathway that looked fresh, but he could not locate the elephants. He saw a small herd of zebra in the distance, and that was all.

He wondered what Mutisya was feeling, standing next to him in his old khaki shorts and a torn white undershirt. Mutisya did not know exactly how old he was, but he figured his age as about forty. His black face was smooth and unlined; the muscles in his bare legs were long and powerful. There was something enduring about Mutisya: he had been here before Royce came and he would be here after Royce was gone. He was a Kamba, as were all of the men who worked for the Baboonery; his incisors were filed down to points in the old tribal fashion. He was a good man, with the gift of dignity. Royce wished him well, whatever the future might hold for him.

The Land Rover approached the drop-off that masked the valley of the Tsavo. Kilatya stopped without being told. It was possible to drive all the way to the river when the country was dry, but the game there spooked easily. It was better to walk.

The three men walked quietly to the rim of the valley. The river seemed very near; it was in fact no more than three-quarters of a mile away. It looked placid and still from where they were, like a dark ribbon of oil. Actually, the water in the Tsavo was clear and the current was fairly swift. Africans drank from it all the time, but Royce had never tried it. He stuck to water that had been boiled and filtered.

Royce lifted his glasses and surveyed the valley. There was a good deal of vegetation and there were even patches of green here and there. He picked up the giraffes first, off to his right. There were a lot of them, sixteen or seventeen that he could count. He swung the glasses and saw a troop of baboons out on the rocks by the river with one big old male standing guard. He wasted no time on them. He saw all the baboons he needed while he was working. He moved the glasses to his left.

There they were.

Four of them that he could see. No, five. Waterbucks.

He studied them closely, his palms beginning to sweat. They were all males. There was something about waterbucks that got to him; it was just one of those things. They weren't very good eating and most hunters thought little of them. But the waterbuck was a majestic animal. They were big fellows; there wasn't an animal in the group that was much under four hundred pounds. They held their heads erect with their annulated horns almost motionless. They had a white ring around their rumps and patches of snowy white at their throats and eyes. Their coats were a gray-brown with a pronounced reddish tint.

He looked at them intently but he did not see Buck. Buck was one in a million, an old bull that moved with the grace of a legend. He would hit five hundred pounds easily. Buck would be a record if he could get him, but it wasn't the record that challenged Royce. Buck was . . . special. There is always one animal that stands as a symbol for a hunter, one animal that consummates the dream. For Royce, it was Buck. He had only seen him twice. Buck did not run with a herd, but he had been near groups of males when Royce had seen him.

There was always a chance.

"Come on," he said.

He started to walk into the valley. Mutisya came along without comment, but Kilatya hesitated. Royce turned and beckoned. Kilatya was a good tracker. Kilatya held back but finally came after them. He seemed very nervous.

They walked down into the shadowed valley of the Tsavo, bearing to the left. It was very still. The soft call of a dove accentuated the silence. The dove called in a regular pattern, first two short calls and then a pause, and then four slightly longer calls with an emphasis on the next to last one. It sounded almost like an owl: hoo hoo . . . hoo hoo *hoo* hoo.

Royce checked his watch. Five-thirty. They didn't have much time left now.

It was the killing time for the big cats.

In fifteen minutes they were out on the valley floor and the ridge from which they had come was dark behind them. Royce had seen nothing: nothing had moved. He could not see the waterbucks now. He could see the heads and stalk-necks of the giraffes in the distance and that was all.

Then, quite suddenly, he heard something.

The sound was not loud but it was . . . disturbing. It was out of place. It did not belong.

A humming noise, like a great generator. A faint whistling roar, not an animal's cry, almost beyond the threshold of hearing . . .

He looked up, trying to find the source of the sound. He saw, or thought he saw, an arc of white in the cloud-shadowed sky. It was like a phantom vapor trail but it did not persist. He had just a glimpse of it, curving down toward the earth, and then it vanished.

He held his breath and listened. There was nothing. No sound of a crash, certainly. Even the humming was gone.

The fading sun lost its warmth. Royce felt cold. The thing might have been a jet, certainly; the big planes sometimes passed over this area. And yet, somehow, he could not believe it. He had seen and heard plenty of jets and this one was *wrong*.

Whatever it was, it had come down near the Baboon-ery. If it had been anything at all . . .

Buck had been shoved out of his mind. It was getting late. Night would fall before they could get back to Kathy and the kids.

He led Mutisya and Kilatya back up the ridge to the Land Rover, moving almost at a trot. All three men got into the cab. It was crowded but Royce was grateful for the nearness of the other men.

Royce punched the starter. The engine caught on the second try. He switched on the lights and turned the Land Rover around. He picked up the trail and got moving. He hit forty, which was too fast for the road.

It was pitch dark when they reached the steep Kikumbuliu crossing. Royce had a bad moment going up the bank but the four wheels dug in and pulled the vehicle over. He yanked the red-knobbed lever and went back into two-wheel drive. The worst was over now.

He drove through the thick bush and he could feel the darkness pressing in around him. The twin beams of the headlights were like toy flashlights in a sea of black. He felt a momentary sense of panic, a drowning in an ocean of night, a sensation of shadows that were reaching out for him, swallowing him. . . .

They came out of the bush. The clearing was startling in its openness, its familiar solidity. He saw the warm lights of the Baboonery ahead of him.

He knew at once that nothing was wrong. He shook his head. He was getting jumpy, acting like a child afraid of the dark. Maybe he had been out here too long.

He drove the Land Rover past the baboon cages and stopped it under a floodlight that was some forty yards behind the barracks where the African staff lived. They unloaded the stiffening kudu and Royce gave Mutisya instructions to relay to Elijah, the foreman. The kudu had to be butchered without delay and the meat stored in the freezer.

Royce moved the Land Rover to its usual parking

place at the back of the main building. He got out and took the keys with him. He was very tired.

He didn't know what to tell Kathy. Had anything really happened? Kathy was not the nervous type, but he did not want to alarm her over nothing. Better wait, he decided. If she had not noticed anything peculiar he could take a look around tomorrow. For what, he did not know.

He looked up at the stars blazing in the great night sky. Then slowly, almost reluctantly, he looked out into the bush. The lights of the Baboonery were only a fragile island in a sea of darkness. The vastness of the African night lapped at the edges of the light, trying to get in.

Royce felt very much alone.

Even as he stood there, the drums started up from somewhere near the railroad. Royce smiled a little. It was nothing more than a dance over at Kikumbuliu Station. Still, he could have done without the drums tonight. The world did not seem as neatly predictable as it once had.

He took a firm grip on his .375 and went inside to eat his dinner.

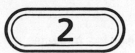

2

ROYCE WOKE UP the next morning to the sound of excited voices. There was no shouting, nothing alarming. Just a babble of voices drifting through the open window. Ordinarily, the sound would not have been enough to awaken him. He must have been tense, he thought, sleeping on the edge . . .

He sat up straight in the bed, instantly alert. Kathy stirred drowsily at his side.

"What's going on?" she muttered into her pillow.

Royce strained to make some sense out of the voices. Everyone seemed to be talking at once. They were all speaking in Kamba, which didn't help any. Royce's knowledge of Swahili left something to be desired but his Swahili was better than his Kamba. He did catch the word *nguli*. Baboon.

"Just some problem with the monkeys," he said. "Go on back to sleep. The kids are still out cold."

He piled out of bed, jerked on his pants and a shirt,

19

and slipped his bare feet into some scuffed loafers. He left the bedroom at a moderately civilized pace and closed the door behind him. He hesitated a moment at the gun safe on the breezeway, decided that he did not need a weapon, and ran outside.

The men were all gathered in a knot over by the baboon cages. The baboons had caught the air of excitement and were very active, banging around in their cages and making explosive coughing noises. Royce had heard that sound many times in his work with baboons—it sounded exactly like the noise a man would make if you crept up behind him and stuck a big, dull knife in his back. There was a strong smell of urine.

Royce joined the men. The reason for all the commotion was plain enough. Two of the sturdy baboon cages had been ripped open. One cage was empty. In the other one there was a male baboon—a big fellow weighing some fifty pounds—dead on the floor of the cage. His great white teeth were exposed in a snarl of pain. He looked as though he had been torn apart. One leg had been wrenched from its socket; it was attached to the animal only by a strip of bloody hide.

Royce reached into the cage and dragged the body out. The animal lay stiffly on the hard-packed earth. The baboon was not a lovely animal at best, and he looked worse in death. He was somehow an obscene, snouted, four-footed caricature of a human being, and the analogy was not lost on Royce.

"Well, Elijah, what do you make of it?"

Elijah Matheka, the headman, shrugged. His eyes,

behind the tinted glasses he always wore, were very wide. "One is dead, one is gone. That is all I know, Mr. Royce."

"You heard nothing?"

"None of us heard anything. When we got up it was just as you saw it."

Royce crouched down and fingered the body. There were no puncture wounds that he could see. The skull was intact; there was no fracture. The animal looked as if something had grabbed it and literally pulled it apart. And something—or someone—had forced the cages open.

A man? It would take a man of extraordinary strength, to say nothing of stupidity. Royce would no more have gone after a baboon with his bare hands than he would have wrestled an elephant. No one from outside would have bothered, unless he had been dead drunk. Baboons were worthless except for research. The men on the place had no great love for baboons, and the feeling was reciprocated. They were not above poking a stick at a troublesome animal, or even shaving a patch of his hide when he was out cold so that the bugs could get at him better. But they had never killed a baboon here. It was senseless. If they lost one they had trapped they just had to trap another one, and that was too much like work.

"Mutisya. Any tracks?"

"I did not see any. The ground here is very hard."

Royce stood up. He felt quite calm, which he recognized as his reaction to trouble. He knew that this incident, whatever its meaning, was only the beginning. There had to be a reason behind it. It could not be written off as just one of those things. He had to find that reason.

If troubles were coming, it was bad policy to get the men all stirred up.

He had not forgotten what he had seen and heard the day before. He could think of no connection, but it disturbed him.

"Okay," he said. "We'll have to keep our eyes open for awhile. Elijah, please take that baboon and put it in the freezing compartment in the operating room. Don't forget to switch on the freezer. The police may want to have a look at it. Mutisya, take Kilatya along with you and see if you can find any tracks out along the edges of the bush. Just walk in a big circle, understand? If you don't find anything, we'll check the traps as usual later. All clear?"

The two Africans nodded.

Royce turned and started back to the main building. He eyed it with a strange sensation of never having seen it before. It was a long rectangular structure built on piles. The walls were of unpainted boards, slightly golden in the morning sun. The roof was gray thatch. At one end was his bedroom, where Kathy and the children were asleep. Next came the screened breezeway, with the concrete gun safe set against one side. The next room was the kitchen, the biggest room in the building. It was a pleasant place, with its great wood-burning stove and gleaming white refrigerator and freezer. He noted with approval that there was a curl of blue smoke drifting up into the pale sky; Wathome would have the coffee ready soon. After the kitchen came the combined dining room and sitting room: a long plank table with wooden chairs, some uncomfortable leather-covered furniture, a radio, a pocked dart board. Finally, at the far end of the main building, next to the dirt road, there was a guest bedroom.

It was all very familiar, and very odd. Africa was like that, he thought. It was a real place, not just a squiggle on a map. Like any real place, it had its share of monotony, of boredom, of the commonplace. There were times when he had to remind himself of where he was. *Hey, I'm in Africa!* There were times when he had to look up and out, look far to the westward, where he could sometimes see the snow-capped twin peaks of Kilimanjaro suspended in the clouds.

And there were times when he sensed sharply where he was, and what he was. A stranger in a land that could be suddenly alien. A man surrounded by a world that was not always what it seemed, a world still half understood.

Well, the baboons had settled one thing.

He would have to tell Kathy.

Kathy looked up when he came in. She was still in bed, but the kids were awake. Susan, who was eight, was already dressed. Barbara, who had just turned five, was tugging on her shorts.

"What was that all about?" Kathy asked.

"That's a good question. Tell you all about it after breakfast, okay?"

"But what happened? Did a baboon bite Elijah or was it the other way around?"

"After breakfast."

She caught the note of strain in his voice. "Okay. You're the *bwana*."

He gave Susan a pat on her close-cropped hair; they had to keep the kids' hair short to frustrate the bugs. "You and Barbara run along to the kitchen and ask Wathome to give you your breakfast. Daddy's going to shave."

The children ran out happily enough. They got a big charge out of eating with Wathome, and already their Swahili was better than Royce's.

There was a silence in the room after the kids had gone and Royce didn't break it. He went into the bathroom and took his time about shaving. There wasn't any hot water yet; the water was heated in a pipe attached to the kitchen stove and it didn't really warm up until around noon. Royce was in no hurry. He needed time to think.

He came out, sat down on the bed, and kissed his wife. Her body was still warm with sleep.

"What was that for?" she asked.

"Just felt like it."

She looked at him. "There *is* something wrong, isn't there?"

"Maybe." Royce hadn't gotten married yesterday. There was a right time for discussing problems, and that time was definitely not in the morning before your wife was fully awake. "Let's get some coffee in us and we'll hash it out. I'll go and ride herd on Wathome—I don't want any of that pineapple and mush for breakfast this morning."

Kathy slipped out of bed. "Be with you in a minute."

Royce went into the kitchen, checked to see that Susan and Barbara were messing gleefully with their corn flakes, and told Wathome to fry up some bacon and eggs.

He poured himself a cup of black coffee from the big pot on the stove and took it into the dining room.

He finished the coffee before Kathy joined him and had another cup with his breakfast. The eggs were greasy and the bacon was tough and on the rancid side. He said nothing of consequence until Kathy had finished her second cup of coffee.

"Well?" she said.

Royce fired up his pipe and chose his words with some care. He told her exactly what had happened. He neither exaggerated nor minimized it. He told her about his feeling of being watched, the thing he had seen and heard in the sky, and the two baboons, one missing and one dead. "I don't know what the hell is going on," he said. "Some of it could just be my imagination. But that baboon is real enough. I'm worried, and *that's* real enough."

"I don't like you spending so much time out there in the bush," Kathy said slowly. "If something is really happening, you could just disappear and I'd never know what became of you."

Royce knocked out his pipe. "I can take care of myself. But I can't stay here all the time and do my job. That's the problem. What happens if there's trouble here while I'm gone?"

"I'm not alone here. The men would take care of me."

"Maybe. I hope so."

He studied his wife. Kathy had been a pretty girl when he had married her ten years before, but now, at thirty, she was more than pretty. Not beautiful, if by beauty you meant the blank-faced androids that sleep-walked through the movies or the curious mammals that posed in the boys' magazines. Kathy had been marked by living. Her body was a bit softened by the two children she had carried. There were tiny wrinkles at the corners of her brown eyes, but the eyes were still alive; the fun had not gone out of them. Kathy flew off the handle sometimes, but never over big things. Like many women, she was at her best in a crisis.

"Honey, I'm wondering if you shouldn't maybe take the kids and fly home, just for a few months. Until we find out what the score is."

Kathy laughed. "For a dead baboon? Leave you here all alone? You'd forget to take your malaria pills. You'd marry a Kamba girl and I'd never see you again. That's out. If I go, you go."

"Damn it, this isn't funny."

"I didn't say it was. But if it's serious enough to send me away then you haven't got any business being here either. You can't have it both ways."

"We've got to be practical. I can't leave. This is one of the most isolated spots on the face of the earth. If there is trouble I might not be able to get you out in time."

"Has anyone threatened you? Or me? Or the kids?"

"No. Not yet."

"Then why can't we just wait and see? We talked this all out before we came here. I'm not going to run home at the first sign of trouble. Isn't Donaldson coming in with a safari today?"

"Today or tomorrow."

"He'll camp right down the road there, won't he, like he always does? That should give us some protection, if we need it."

"I'd hate to trust my wife to the tender care of Matt Donaldson. He's a peculiar guy, Kathy."

"You've got romantic white hunters on the brain, dear. I couldn't care less about Donaldson as a man—but he knows this country and he knows guns. He'd be a good man to have around if anything happened."

Royce stood up. He felt vaguely annoyed that Kathy did not share the unease he felt. He could not put the thing into words. Something in the sky, a dead baboon, a missing baboon. It was absurd. And yet . . .

"Okay," he said. "We'll let it ride awhile. But I want you to take the .38 out of the gun safe and put it in the bedroom. If something happens, you take the kids, go in there, and lock the door. If you have to shoot, shoot to kill. Don't close your damn eyes."

"What am I supposed to shoot? A baboon? A Mau Mau?"

"Or Frankenstein's monster. Or a lust-crazed white hunter. Hell, *I* don't know. But I'm not kidding, Kathy. You take that .38 and you get it ready."

"Yes, *bwana*. I love you when you're masterful."

"Good. After I run the trap line, I may stop in and have a talk with Bob Russell. Maybe he has some ideas. I'll send Elijah into Mitaboni to notify the police. They won't do anything but maybe they'll send a man out here to look at that baboon. I'll be back before dark."

At that moment, Susan ran **in**. She jumped up and

down in great joy. "Barby just had a BM in her pants," she announced proudly.

Kathy got up. "Life goes on," she said.

Royce went to get his rifle out of the gun safe. He supposed that kids had gone on having bowel movements in the middle of Mau Mau raids, or Indian raids for that matter, but it certainly seemed inappropriate.

He forced himself to start thinking about the traps he had to check.

It was a strange world. At a time like this his wife had to change Barby's pants and he had to go off to hunt baboons.

Still, as Kathy said, life went on.

Royce took Mutisya with him in the Land Rover. Mutisya had found no tracks in his search around the Baboonery. In itself, that was not too peculiar. The land was very hard after the long dry spell and it did not take tracks easily, not even elephant tracks.

They took the back trail, the one that ran along the railroad for a few miles, crossed the Tsavo where the river was low enough, and wound up in Mitaboni. The traps were on the far side of the Tsavo; Royce wanted to work that area before the rains came. Nobody could get into that place during the rainy season.

Even if there had been no traps, Royce would have taken this trail. If something *had* fallen from the sky, it must have been in this general region. The thought crossed his mind that it might have been a space capsule of some sort. He had been told that some of the early

astronauts had passed right over the Baboonery. Even the
moon shots involved some earth orbits. He had not heard
of any new launchings, but he supposed that there were
experiments with both manned and unmanned craft that
were not announced to the public. Surely, though, if there
had been trouble the area would be crawling with people.
He hadn't even seen a search plane.

He kept his eyes open nevertheless.

Unhappily, there was little to see. The land was flat
under the great blue sky, flat and red and parched. No
Kamba lived here and there were few animals visible. The
monotony was broken only by the gray baobabs, looking
like Disney trees with their fat trunks and spindly
branches, and by the euphorbia plants, which were cactuslike and always reminded Royce of the sort of thing
people expected to see in Texas but which would have
been more at home in California or Arizona. The sun was
hot and the Land Rover kicked up thick clouds of red dust.
The dust was half an inch thick on the floor of the Land
Rover before they had gone two miles.

They crossed the Tsavo at the ford with only the usual
difficulties of slipping wheels and water through the floor-
boards. Royce had been informed that there were croco-
diles in the Tsavo, but apparently they were not as
mindlessly aggressive as they were in the movies. He had
never seen one. On the far side of the river the vegetation
was thicker and the flies and mosquitoes were a nuisance.
Royce remembered that he had forgotten to take his
daraprim that morning and made a mental note to swallow the pill when he got back. Once a week, and it was all

too easy to forget. Malaria had a way of reminding a man if he forgot too often.

It was early afternoon when they reached the clearing where the traps were set. Baboons were all over the place when they arrived, even climbing on the traps themselves. The animals pulled back at the sight of the Land Rover but they did not go far. There were about fifty of them and most of them took to the trees. This had surprised Royce the first time he had seen it; baboons were ground-dwelling monkeys and they liked open country and rocks. The books all said that they weren't much good in the trees, but evidently the baboons had read the wrong books. They frisked about like so many giant squirrels, and they made a fearful din.

Royce ignored them. He knew from experience that the troop would stay close and holler in an attempt to frighten him away from the trapped animals, but the baboons would not attack. It was strictly a bluff.

He pulled the Land Rover up to the first traps and stopped. He climbed out, leaving the rifle in the vehicle. He took the gadget he always thought of as a prod pole with him. It was not actually a prod, being basically a syringe attached to a wooden pole about four feet long.

There was no need to speak. He and Mutisya had the routine down pat by now.

There were three traps in the first series and two of them held baboons. The third trap was sprung but the animal had gotten away. Royce studied the empty trap with some care. The traps were quite simple. They were just big cages made out of wood and wire with a raised platform in the center. The bait, usually pineapple or maize, was fastened to the platform by a cord. When the baboon climbed up and moved the food, a trigger was released that dropped the door of the cage. That was that, unless the baboon managed to force the wire enough to get out. A large baboon was a powerful animal; there had been escapes before. Royce could not tell whether the empty trap had been opened from within or without. He saw nothing suspicious, but it did seem to him that if someone were swiping baboons this would be the place to come. Why go to the Baboonery where there were people around?

The two caged baboons were alarmed and wary. They were also dangerous. They rushed around the cages in a panic, lunging at the wire and snapping their impressive jaws. They made very rapid coughing noises and thoughtfully dropped sticky dung all over the cage floors.

Royce eliminated one right away; she was a female, and his current orders called for only males within a weight range of thirty to fifty pounds. She would have to be released, but not until they had gotten the baboons they needed.

The other one was okay.

"Friend," Royce said, "how would you like to visit the United States?"

The baboon did not seem enthusiastic.

Royce approached him with care. A trapped baboon was a formidable animal. They were very large for monkeys, bigger than the smallest ape, the gibbon. They had nasty dispositions when they were crossed, and they were tough. Royce had seen war dogs in action, but he had often thought that they couldn't hold a candle to a war baboon if there had been such a thing. Unlike most monkeys, the baboon was not flat-faced. Possibly because of his terrestrial habits, he had a tremendous projecting snout. He had powerful jaws liberally supplied with strong white teeth, and he knew how to use them. Once a baboon caught hold of an arm or a leg it was almost impossible to pry his jaws open. There had been accidents at the Baboonery and Royce had learned to keep his mind on what he was doing.

He filled the syringe on the end of the pole with sernyl. Mutisya went around to the back of the cage and attracted the animal's attention. Royce made one quick lunge, got the needle in the baboon's rump, and rammed the elongated plunger home. The baboon shrieked, whirled, and rushed across the cage. Royce stepped back out of range.

There was nothing to do now but wait. Knocking out a freshly trapped baboon was not particularly difficult. It was a nightmare, though, when you had to knock them out a second time at the Baboonery, or if you chanced to catch a baboon that had been stuck before but had escaped. The animals were quick to learn, and they wanted no part of that needle a second time. They would grab at the needle when it came into the cage and they were so fast that they could twist the needle off before you could get it out of range again. Royce had once spent three solid hours trying to stick a baboon in a small cage without success.

The animal showed no instant effects from the sernyl,

but he gradually slowed his desperate lunging. Within minutes, his eyes turned glassy and he began to stagger. The snarl on his face relaxed into what closely resembled a bemused smile. He hauled himself up onto the platform, wobbled on rubber legs for a moment, and fell in a heap to the floor of the cage.

Royce gave him another minute, then opened the cage. He dragged the inert body by the legs to the Land Rover and dumped the baboon into the back of the vehicle. The animal would be out cold for several hours, and they could give him another shot if necessary. Occasionally, they miscalculated and a baboon revived ahead of schedule. Royce had fond memories of the day when a big animal had come to in the market at Mitaboni and had staggered out on a tour of inspection. It had been great fun for awhile, but it was not really dangerous. The baboons had a bit of a hangover when they first revived, and they were slow and easy to catch.

They checked all of the traps in the clearing, and when they were through they had four baboons sleeping the good sleep in the back of the Land Rover. They released eleven animals, all of them females or immature specimens. They repaired and reset the traps. Next time, Royce knew, they would be less successful. Most of the baboons would be wary now and stay clear of the traps. Soon, Royce would have to bring in a crew and shift the traps to a new location. That was a hard job and he was not looking forward to it.

The two men climbed back in the Land Rover and Royce continued along the trail to Mitaboni. He saw nothing that was in any way unusual but the nagging sense of unease persisted. Royce knew that he was driving too fast; the limp baboons were bouncing in the back.

There was something very funny going on, something he could not understand. The unknown was always a potential threat. Whatever it was, it could be dangerous.

It would not just go away.

He wanted to talk to Bob Russell.

If anyone could help him, it would be Russell.

3

H E DROVE THROUGH Mitaboni without stopping, a
process that took less than thirty seconds. Mitaboni
didn't amount to much, and the first time Royce had seen
it he had reacted with something close to despair. With
time, however, Mitaboni took on a certain charm.

Mitaboni was like a lot of the little towns that had
grown up in Africa during the past fifty years. It was a
shipping point for the railroad, with a series of large cattle
pens strung out along the track on the northern end of the
settlement. It was a minor stopping place on the main road
from Nairobi to Mombasa, boasting two petrol stations.
One was Shell and the other was Ozo, and both of them
ran a kind of general store on the side. There were no
Europeans in Mitaboni, and most of the shops were still
run by Asians. The ubiquitous Patel boys controlled the
Shell station, and one Dalip Singh was the Ozo im-
presario. The buses used Mitaboni as a watering stop,
pulling in several times a day to disgorge loads of sweating

and irritable passengers in search of soft drinks. There was a small open-air African market, a shack called the Corner Bar which did a fair business in Tusker beer, a rather pretty old mosque, and a shed that served as a post office. It was one of the miracles of the ages that a letter mailed in that post office eventually reached the United States; Royce had never lost any mail, coming or going. There was a grim looking hotel that had been patronized mainly by Asians whose cars had broken down on the punishing road; now that the road had been paved after a fashion it had lost most of its business. Europeans who wanted to stop on the road between Nairobi and Mombasa always stopped at the oasis of Hunter's Lodge, some twenty miles away on the Nairobi side, or at Mac's Inn, about thirty miles distant toward Mombasa. Mitaboni also boasted a tiny whitewashed police station, staffed with three African members of the Kenya Police who spent most of their time cruising about with great dignity on bicycles.

Royce relaxed a little when he had cleared Mitaboni and was out on the main road. It was a genuine pleasure to get away from the thick dust and the jarring jolts. He could hit sixty with safety now that he knew where the worst holes were.

He drove eight miles toward Mombasa—and also toward the Baboonery—and then turned off to the left down the well-kept dirt road that led to Russell's house. One nice thing about the main road was that you always knew exactly where you were. There were stake markers placed every mile along the way. On one side they gave the mileage to Mombasa, and on the other the mileage to Nairobi. Russell's turnoff was at mile 140 on the Mombasa side.

It took him several minutes to reach the house and he could hear the dogs barking long before he got there. Russell's land was mostly planted in sisal; it was too dry to grow most of the profitable cash crops. It was not lush and green like the farms in the highlands—those that were left—but Russell made up the difference in quantity. He had thousands of acres and he used them well.

The house was a substantial one, a low rambling structure of white stone and stained wood. A great porch lined one whole side of the building, and Russell had screened it in against the bugs.

Royce stopped the Land Rover and before he could get out Russell had come outside to greet him. Royce asked Mutisya to check the baboons and give them another shot if they started to come around. Then he went on alone to talk to Russell. He could have taken Mutisya with him, but it would have been awkward with an old settler. Russell's men would see to it that Mutisya got something to eat and drink. The system was changing, but it still made Royce uncomfortable. While he was Russell's guest he would have to play it Russell's way.

Bob Russell was a short, chunky man, but he was not fat. He was as hard as though he had been cast from iron. His broad face was very red, partly from sunburn and partly from many years of close attention to a gin bottle. His hair was long and straight and jet black, and he brushed it back without a part. His eyes, under bushy black brows, were shrewd and very dark. He was dressed in the standard Kenya uniform: white shirt with the sleeves rolled up, khaki shorts that were baggy by American standards, sturdy black shoes with tan socks that came almost up to his knobby knees.

He stuck out his broad, hard hand and Royce took it. "Well, Crawford," he said. "Good timing, if I may say so. I was just about to have tea. Hope you can join me?"

"Thanks. I'd appreciate it very much."

"Not at all. Always glad to see you. Gets a bit lonely out here, you know. Come in, come in."

Royce followed him across the porch and into the main sitting room. It was wonderfully cool in the house and spotlessly clean. The room was big and comfortable. It had no frills, but it was as solid and pleasant a room as Royce had ever been in. There were worn zebra-skin rugs on the red tile floor and a very fine kudu head was hung on the wall over the great fireplace. The couches and chairs were faded but substantial; they looked like they were good for another fifty years. There were only three pictures in the room, photographs that stood in matching frames on a long side table. One was of Russell's wife, who had died nine years ago. The others were of his sons, both of whom were in England. Shelves lined two walls and they were filled with books. The books were a wild assortment ranging from British paperbacks to large leather-bound works on African exploration in the old days. Most of the Kenya settlers had been great readers, there being very little else to do on the remote farms when the day's work was done, but Russell was exceptional. He read omnivorously and he could discuss anyone from Shakespeare to Sartre. There was an ancient grandfather clock in one corner, taller than a man, and its unhurried ticking filled the room with the measured beats of eternity.

Russell's houseboy, a lanky African dressed in the traditional *kanzu* that looked like a cotton nightshirt, padded in on bare feet and waited for instructions. He knew perfectly well what the order would be, but that was part of the ritual.

"*Chai kwa mbili*," Russell said. "*Upesi!*"

Royce stifled a smile. He had a vision of a couple of straw-hatted soft-shoe men dancing out on a stage while the band struck up that old favorite, "*Chai kwa Mbili*" — better known in some quarters as "*Tea for Two*."

The two men made small talk until the tea arrived, and Royce found it heavy going. Unlike most of the Englishmen he had known, Russell made him feel somewhat uncomfortable. The man was cordial enough in a superficial sort of way, but he had a trick of keeping his distance. Royce had a notion that Russell resented him, resented his presence in Kenya. The feeling was understandable enough. Bob Russell had been here, on this farm, for thirty-five years. He had built this house. He had carved his sisal plantation out of the bush, and he had fought rhinos and elephants and malaria and God knew what to do it. He had lived through the time of the Mau Mau and the difficulties that had come with independence. He had lost his wife to this land. His future was uncertain. And now an American breezed in on a jet, took a cushy job trapping baboons, and made more money than he did. It gave a man food for thought.

Still, most of the English were not like that, not the

ones Royce had met. Whoever had dreamed up the stereotype of the cold reserved Englishman had not spent much time in Kenya—or in England either, for that matter. Perhaps he was not being fair to Russell. The man had had a tough time of it. In any event, he was the only settler who lived anywhere near the Baboonery. If Russell couldn't tell him what he needed to know, then he was not likely to get the information anywhere else.

Tea time was a ceremony, of course, and it could not be rushed. The African brought out a silver tray with two small pots of tea, two fine china cups and saucers, sugar, a pitcher of milk, cakes, cookies, and a variety of tiny rectangular sandwiches—cheese, cucumber, and lettuce. It took Royce half an hour to do justice to the ritual. He pulled out his pipe and lit it. Russell fished out a cigarette and inhaled deeply. He smoked Rex, a local brand of filter-tips.

Royce could now come to the point.

"I've run into something strange at the Baboonery," he said. "I'd appreciate getting your advice on it."

"Ah. Well, let's have a crack at it."

Royce told him what had happened. The story seemed overly familiar now; it was the second time he had gone through it that day. It was difficult to communicate a sense of urgency.

Russell lit another cigarette, watching Royce intently. "That's all there is? You have left nothing out?"

"That's it."

"Well, now. You have two problems, it seems, or maybe three. What was it that you saw in the sky? What could kill a baboon like that? And what would want to steal a baboon? It sounds rather like something out of Conan Doyle."

"You know this country. Does any of this ring a bell?"

Russell thought it over carefully. "It *is* strange. It's a big sky we have here, you know. I've seen things in my time. Meteorites, fireballs—something of the sort most likely. As for the baboons, I haven't a clue. Fifteen years or so ago, yes. You weren't here during the Emergency, of course. That sort of thing wasn't at all uncommon then. Dogs skewered on gateposts, cattle with their heads cut off, all that sort of rot. But there aren't any Mau Mau these days—they're all in the bloody government." His voice was edged with bitterness, the helpless anger of a man left behind by the retreat of empire. He paused a moment and went on more calmly. "That's all over and done with. Things have worked out better than I thought they would, I'll give Kenyatta that. Doesn't help with *your* problem, though. Almost has to be a man. What else could it be?"

"How could a man tear a baboon apart that way? And why bother? Why not just shoot an arrow into him?"

"I've no idea. Why do Africans do anything? I'll tell you this, Crawford. This is an old country, Africa. Birthplace of man and all that, if old Leakey is right about those skeletons of his. Empires rose and fell on this continent when England was just a pack of wild men. There are ancient currents here, currents that you and I will never understand. You take our Kamba friends. They look harmless enough now, and some idiots even find them comical. But these people fought the Masai to a standstill, and they once had a trading network that controlled a territory all the way from the Indian Ocean to Lake Victoria. People don't change completely overnight, Crawford. I know all about the schools and the ministers and the judges. I give them their due. But I know all about the witchcraft and the killing oaths and the poisoned arrows, too. These people have one foot in another world. You can't figure them out. Don't try."

"But look, Bob. You don't rip a baboon apart with witchcraft. Maybe the Kamba were responsible. There's some resentment toward the Baboonery. It probably won't be many years before the government has to chop it up into farms. But what kind of a Kamba is it who can do that to a baboon with his bare hands?"

"A drunk one," Russell suggested.

"I just can't believe it," Royce said reluctantly. "I wish I could."

Russell shrugged. "You haven't been harmed yet. Stay out of it. Keep your eyes open. Look out for your own business, do your own job. You asked for my opinion. I'm afraid that's it. Not very helpful, I suppose. You don't have to go out of your way looking for trouble in this country. It will find you if it's headed your way."

Royce stood up. "I appreciate your advice. I'll think on it. I'd better be getting back now."

"Care for a quick one before you go? Dusty road ahead of you, you know."

"Thanks, but I don't want to leave Kathy there after dark alone. Another time, if I may. You must drop in and see us soon. Donaldson should be in with a safari shortly. Drive over and we'll break out a fifth."

"Sounds good. I might do that." Russell extended his hard, blunt hand. "Be careful. And keep me informed, will you?"

"Right. Thanks again."

Royce hurried out to the Land Rover. "Okay, Mutisya?"

"Okay, Mr. Royce."

Royce drove back to the main road and pushed the vehicle as fast as he dared toward the little trail that angled off to the Baboonery. He covered the nine miles in eight minutes, which was pretty good. He turned off to the right where the old white sign was nailed to the baobab tree: *Kikumbuliu Station*. There was no mention of the Baboonery, which was beyond the station on the other side of the railroad track.

He had to slow down to a crawl. It was ten miles to the Baboonery and the road was nothing more than a rough dirt track hacked through the bush.

The sun was low in the red-tinged sky. The desiccated bush was hot and still. The gritty red dust was everywhere, like the patina of ages covering a landscape of the dead. There was no sign of life except for a single dik-dik, no larger than a dog, that sprang up in the middle of the road and ran away at the sound of the Land Rover's approach.

He passed the deserted loading shed that marked the station and bounced across the railroad track, those incongruous strips of battered metal that lanced an improbable hole through the African wilderness. It had taken more than a few lives to lay those tracks. The so-called man-eaters of Tsavo sounded rather melodramatic by today's standards, but the big cats had been real enough. He pushed on toward the Baboonery. The road was even worse now, if possible. It had taken him nearly an hour to cover the ten miles from the main road.

He saw them as soon as he reached the edge of the clearing.

Kathy was sitting on the wooden steps outside the main sitting room, watching Susan and Barbara playing in the dirt.

She waved to him.

Royce felt a sudden stab of relief and noticed that his hands were trembling on the wheel.

It had been a long day.

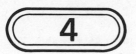

4

THE NEXT MORNING started out like a repeat of the day before. One of the cages had been broken open and another baboon was gone.

At first, Royce was more angry than worried. The theft seemed a calculated affront, an insult rather than a threat. He had set up a watch during the night and the loss of another baboon was galling.

"Well, Elijah," he said to his headman. "This was your responsibility. Who was on duty last night?"

"Kilatya, Mr. Royce." Elijah's eyes were invisible behind his tinted glasses.

"And where is Kilatya? What does he have to say?"

"Kilatya, he says nothing. He is not here."

"Where the hell is he?"

"I do not know. He is not here."

Royce put his hands on his hips. "That's just great."

He knew that there was no point in questioning the other men. Even if they knew where Kilatya was they would not tell him. It was not unusual for a man to disappear for a day or two and then show up again with some unlikely but immensely detailed explanation. Royce had learned to accept the stories with good grace and simply dock the man a day's wages. The alternative was to have no crew at all. Kilatya was a fine tracker; Royce needed him.

In this case, it was not difficult to figure out what had happened. Kilatya had been standing guard and he had lost a baboon. Rather than face the music, he had gone home to hide. He would probably be back eventually.

The fact remained that another baboon had been taken. Royce spent the morning checking for signs. He found one place with some broken brush and a sharp-edged depression that looked as though it had been made by a heavy object—the sort of mark that might be made by a man taking a large post and ramming it hard against the earth. That was all. There was no trail that he could follow and he was no nearer an explanation than he had been before.

Something was after his baboons. That was the only solid fact that he had, and it made no sense.

Royce had just finished lunch when he heard the trucks coming. He pushed back his plate, which contained the remnants of one of Wathome's favorite concoctions, a grisly mixture of bacon and spaghetti.

"Here comes the great white hunter," he said to Kathy. "Two cheers."

They walked outside and stood on the steps. The

trucks were very close. He could see the billows of red dust that marked their passage. The sun hammered down on the land as though it had a grudge against it. It was hot and still and Royce's shirt was sticking to his back. Nothing green showed anywhere. There was not a cloud in the vast blue sky. The great dry leaves of the banana trees rustled very faintly, reminding him mockingly of the rain that would not come.

The three dust-covered trucks, loaded down with equipment, jolted around the bend in the road. They went on through the Baboonery grounds, showering dust, and turned right toward the Tsavo. Donaldson always camped on the near side of the Kikumbuliu, where the bush opened up after the tsetse fly-infested area.

Royce waited. The Land Rover came along in about five minutes, hanging back to keep free of the dust kicked up by the trucks. Donaldson was at the wheel and he stopped when he saw Royce and Kathy. He jumped out, leaving his clients to stew for a moment in the sun.

"Ho!" he called. "Good to see you again."

He shook hands with both of them. His lean hand was as hard as a rock. Royce stifled his dislike and welcomed him.

Matt Donaldson stood an even six feet but he looked taller than he was. Royce, who topped six feet by three inches, felt short in his presence. Donaldson was lean and sinewy and he moved like a cat. His long hair was the color of straw and his eyebrows were burned to the shade of white gold by the sun. He exuded vitality like a healthy animal. His thin face and his watery blue eyes could be cruel, but he knew how to turn on the charm that was so necessary in his business. He was dressed casually but neatly: khaki shorts and shirt, heavy boots, and a floppy brown hat that he carried in his left hand. The hat was, battered with wear and it was not equipped with a leopard-skin hatband. The dashing hatband was strictly for the hunters who did their stalking in the bars of Nairobi.

"I have a bit of a favor to ask of you, Royce."

"Ask away."

"You remember old Wambua?"

"The political hotshot? I'm not likely to forget him."

"Well, it's like this. The old boy has got wind of the fact that I have a couple of rich American clients out here. He has decided to honor us with his august presence."

Royce groaned. "Another dance?"

Donaldson grinned. "Bang on. He can't be far behind me with his merry men. I have a camp to set up. Will you stop them here and let them get their drums heated up in the clearing in front of your baboon cages? Then we'll come back in a few hours and we'll all watch an exciting, authentic native dance. How does that strike you?"

"You really want to know?"

"I knew you would respond with your customary enthusiasm." Donaldson looked at him closely. "I say, you don't really mind? I *am* in a bit of a spot. . . ."

"Of course not, Matt. Glad to help."

"Thanks so much. Back shortly!"

He trotted back to the Land Rover, climbed in, and gunned the vehicle after the vanished trucks. Royce managed a smile for the two Americans sweating in the front seat.

"There goes a day's work," he said sourly.

"We owe him a few favors," Kathy said. "And we've got to stay on the good side of Wambua. Especially now."

"I'll buy that. Look, I'll tell Elijah to get ready and I'll keep an eye peeled for the *corps de ballet*. You better put the kids down and see if they'll go to sleep this early—they won't be taking any naps once the drumming starts."

He walked off to find Elijah. He was not happy about the loss of time, but he was glad that Donaldson had arrived.

There were times when it was better not to be alone.

The two battered trucks, filled to overflowing with young laughing Africans, clanked into position in front of the baboon cages. The trucks were usually used in hauling produce to various local markets, but Wambua borrowed them occasionally for his dancers. Since Wambua was something of a wheel in the government, the owners of the trucks tended to give them up without undue protest.

The trucks disgorged Africans. All of them, male and female, were quite young. None of them looked over twenty, and some of the girls couldn't have been more than thirteen or fourteen. They were an attractive, healthy-looking group. The men wore shorts, in deference to their European audience, but were barefoot and naked from the waist up. They had on some beads—necklaces, armbands, anklets with rattles—but they weren't dolled up like the girls. The girls wore short black skirts and little beaded bras—again in consideration of what they felt to be proper for a European audience—and they were bedecked in bright-colored beads and rattles. All of the girls had small silver whistles suspended on finely-wrought chains around their necks. Their hair, of course, was cut shorter than the men's.

The dancers went right to work. They got two fires going almost as soon as they left the trucks. The fires weren't just for local color; they needed them to heat the drumheads on the long cylindrical drums, to get them tight enough for proper playing.

Old Wambua came out last and advanced toward Royce. He was a heavy-set man, dressed in a baggy brown European suit with a stained red tie. He carried a fly-whisk as a symbol of his status. He was not really old in years— fifty or sixty perhaps—but he gave an impression of having been around. He bowed slightly and grinned. His front teeth had been filed to sharp points in the old Kamba style.

"*Jambo, Bwana,*" Wambua said. He was kidding, of course; he spoke perfectly good English, and the old deferential Swahili greeting to Europeans was a kind of a joke now.

"*Jambo,*" Royce said, going along with it. "*Karibu, Mutumia.*"

Wambua laughed aloud. Royce had mixed Swahili and Kamba in his reply, telling a tribal elder that he was welcome.

"The two Americans," Wambua said, switching to English. "They are here?"

"In the safari camp with Mr. Donaldson. They'll be along shortly."

Wambua chuckled. "They have much money, very rich. They pay us well for our dance. We make friends for Africans and they see something new. How do you say it? Everyone is triumphant."

"Everybody wins." Of course, they could have seen dancing for nothing almost any night out in the bush. But you had to know where to go, and you had to be careful about cameras. The Africans had the notion that tourists could go back home and make vast sums of money out of their photographs of African dances, and they wanted their cut. Civilization had many facets.

"They come now," Wambua said, nodding.

Royce looked up and saw Matt Donaldson walking along the dirt road from the safari camp. His men apparently had set up the bathing facilities in record time, since the two people with him were no longer covered with trail dust. Royce eyed the Americans without pleasure. Somehow, he always wanted Americans to make a good impression here. The man was young and scrawny, dressed in very tight blue jeans, a fancy new bush jacket of the sort sold at Ahamed's in Nairobi, and a hat with a leopard-skin hatband. The woman with him was a rather striking blonde in a green frock and open-toed sandals. She was puffing on a cigarette in a long black holder.

Donaldson made the introductions and chatted away

glibly about the coming dance, going into his white-hunter-with-incredible-experience routine. "Jolly good, actually. Not up to your Kipsigis, of course, or your Masai. But fascinating, no doubt of that."

Royce managed to swallow that with a straight face. The Masai weren't any great shakes as dancers, and he knew that Matt loathed Kamba dancing. But a hunter had to be more than a crack shot. A good one was a talented bull slinger as well, and Matt Donaldson was one of the best.

Elijah slipped unobtrusively up behind Royce.

Royce turned. "What is it, Elijah?" If the man would only take those tinted glasses off, he thought. It was like talking to a mask.

"I thought you should know, Mr. Royce. Some of these men, these dancers, they are from the place where Kilatya has his wives and his cows. They say he is not there. He has not come home." Elijah waited, shifting from one foot to another—waiting for praise, for instructions, for some indication of what he should do.

Royce could not help him out. He felt chilled by the news; he did not know what it meant. "Thank you, Elijah. There is nothing we can do now. The dance is about to start; you and the rest of the men might as well watch it. We won't be working this afternoon."

"Ndio, Mr. Royce." Elijah looked troubled, but he did not press the matter further. He walked away to join the rest of the African staff, all of whom were already standing in a line to watch the proceedings. Royce's permission to take the afternoon off had been a trifle redundant.

Royce's sense of unease returned very strongly. Something was wrong at the Baboonery. . . .

The Europeans took their seats on folding wooden chairs. (In East Africa, virtually all white men were lumped together as "Europeans." It made little sense to Royce, but that was the way it was.)

The dance began.

To Royce, the most amazing thing about the whole business was the speed with which he had adjusted to it all. He had been at the Baboonery for less than two years, and already he could take the scene before him almost for granted. It took a conscious effort on his part to see the strangeness.

The African bush was all around them, dry as tinder, flaked with red dust, enfolding its secrets under the vast afternoon sky. The world here had been old when man was young, and the animals that prowled through the dead grasses and the sleeping river valleys were very like the ones that men had known thousands of years ago. They were surrounded by miracles of life—the elephant, the lion, the rhino—that were making their last stand against the swelling growth of civilization.

And here, right before their eyes, was a bizarre collection of buildings and people and animals—a cluster of unlikely combinations thrown together as though in defiance of the laws of place and time. Thatched roofs and electricity, drums and radios, trucks and baboons. A professional hunter from England, Americans as different from one another as a Kamba from a Masai, Africans of all kinds: a cook in a *kanzu*, a headman in tinted glasses, a politician in a red tie thinking about an Africa newly born, young people with bare skins gleaming in the sun dancing a traditional dance for money.

There were three drummers, standing on the far side of the dancers. Each had a cylindrical wooden drum about three feet long which was suspended from a thong around the neck and supported on one bent knee. The drumheads were of cowhide or snakeskin, and the drummers played on both ends with the fingers of their hands. The beat was staccato and very fast, rattling out like rifle fire, reaching a crescendo, stopping, and starting again.

The dancers formed two columns with the men on one side and the girls on the other. They did not touch one another. One man faced the dancers, his back to the audience, and shouted out commands like a drill sergeant.

For half an hour or so, the dance was more like a series of rapid marching drills than anything else. The leader would call out his instructions, the drummers would hammer away with a sound like marbles poured out on a hard table, and the two columns would whirl and rush forward and backward with a fair amount of precision. Occasionally, the dancers would raise their hands and make barking noises as though firing imaginary rifles. Each drill was very short, lasting only a few minutes, after which the drums would stop and Wambua would smile benignly and the audience would dutifully applaud.

It got more interesting as the dancers warmed up. The military orders disappeared and the dancing reverted to an older style. Individuals stepped out of the lines and im-

provised dances based on the movements of animals: leap-
ing antelope, pacing ostriches, lumbering rhinos,
trumpeting elephants. The rhythm of the drums became
more complex, with drums beating out counter-rhythms.
The shrill whistles pierced the warm air and the rattles on
the stamping feet added a fourth pattern to the beats of the
drums.

Royce watched, caught up in it now almost in spite of
himself. The Africans in the audience broke up into knots
and began to perform dances of their own.

The dancing girls started to ululate, throwing their
heads back and giving long liquid cries that trembled
through the pulsating noise. The dust thickened and
streaked the gleaming bodies with rivulets of rust.

The dancers paired off, male and female, and the
style of the dance became explicitly sexual. The dancers
still did not touch, but they came very close. First a man
would dance before the girl, then the girl before the man,
and then they would face one another, breathing heavily,
stamping their feet, jerking their heads like turtles back
and forth over the shoulders of their partners.

Money had been the cause of the dance, but money
was forgotten now. The dancers ignored their audience.
They were in a world of their own, a world Royce could
never enter. This was an older Africa, an alien Africa, an
Africa divorced from the world outside. The dance went
on and on until it seemed that the dancers must drop from
sheer exhaustion. The sun dipped into the west and long
shadows crept across the land.

It was dark when the drums stopped. The lights of the

Baboonery were feeble sparks in a night that stretched away to infinity. The sudden silence beneath the emerging stars was taut and explosive.

Royce was emotionally numb. The noise and the dust and the strain had gotten to him. He was dog tired. He kept going somehow until all the visitors were gone. He arranged with Elijah to set up a watch for the night. He ate a cheese sandwich, washed it down with a bottle of beer, and was in bed by nine o'clock.

He slept instantly, but it was a light and troubled sleep.

The drums started up again, somewhere lost in the great African night.

He reached out for Kathy and pulled her close.

Kathy lay awake in his arms, watching the blowing white curtains that fluttered like ghosts on the open windows, listening to the distant drums.

Royce slept late the next morning and he woke up feeling drugged and fuzzy. When he joined Kathy at the breakfast table it took him three cups of violent coffee to get the cotton out of his head.

He noticed that there was something different about the light. He walked to the door and stared out. There were heavy black clouds in the sky, blowing in from the coast of the Indian Ocean. There were still patches of blue and the sun was shining, but the vast vault of the African sky was broken by the drifting mountains of clouds. The wind had freshened, kicking up the red dust, and the air was cooler than it had been for a long time.

"By God," he said. "Look at that."

"It's too early for rain, isn't it?" Kathy asked.

"That's what they say back home just before one of the frog-chokers hits. You're right—the short rains shouldn't start before the end of October. But nothing else in this country operates on schedule. Maybe the short rains are coming three weeks early."

"I don't believe it. It *never* rains here."

"I wouldn't bet on it, sugar."

He stood there, staring at the sky. Unbidden, the memory of what he had seen in that sky crept into his mind. Fireball? Meteorite? Way down deep, he couldn't accept it. It had been something else. . . .

He stepped outside and shaded his eyes. He looked away at the sky, off in the direction of the trapping trail that led to Mitaboni. The lines around his mouth tightened.

"Look at that," he said.

She joined him and followed his pointing finger. She saw them at once and felt a stab of irrational fear she tried to conceal.

The sky was stained with the black dots of birds, hundreds of birds, wheeling in great lazy circles on the wind. The birds were miles away but there was no mistaking them. They were buzzards.

"Maybe Matt took his clients out hunting this morning," she said.

Royce shook his head. "Not there, baby."

He went in and took the .375 from the gun safe. He checked the rifle, stuck some extra shells in his pocket, and climbed into the Land Rover. He picked up Mutisya

and drove as fast as he dared toward where the buzzards
were circling.

Speed was important. Scavengers were notoriously
efficient in Africa.

Something was dead out there. Royce wanted to get a
look at it before it was too late. He tried not to think
beyond that.

It took him nearly an hour of rough, jolting driving.
He had to leave the trail finally and cut across open
country. It was high noon before he reached the kill.

The buzzards took off at his approach, flapping into
the sky with their naked turkey-necks extended like snakes.
He drove right up to the thing on the ground. There were
some twenty obscene marabou storks tearing at the dark
dead figure; they rose heavily into the air, like deacons
with wings, as the Land Rover jerked to a halt. The smell
of death was thick in the sunlight, a smell of meat and
blood and bloated flies.

Royce and Mutisya climbed out of the Land Rover.
They did not speak. They walked over to the body in the
dirt and looked down. Royce's eyes widened in horror. He
swallowed hard to choke back the impulse to vomit.

"Kilatya," he said.

"Yes, Mr. Royce. We have found him."

Royce stared at the thing that had been a man. The
eyes had been pecked out of the skull. One leg was nearly
gone, with the greasy white bone showing through the
strings of flesh. Kilatya's chest, naked to the sky, was
bloody pulp.

An inane phrase kept repeating itself in Royce's

stunned mind. *How about that, sport fans. How about that. . . .*

"Get the tarp from the back of the Land Rover," he said. "We can't pick him up the way he is now."

Mutisya got the tarp. The two men managed to slide the body onto the thick canvas. There was no way to get rid of the flies. They folded the tarp over Kilatya, hiding him, and lifted the body into the back of the Land Rover.

"Mutisya. We must take great care. If there are tracks, we must find them. Understand?"

"*Ndio,* Mr. Royce."

The two men separated, searching the ground. There was no point in looking for signs where the body had been. The birds had messed the place up too much for that. They had to backtrack, find the trail. *Something* had found Kilatya here, and *something* had gone away again. . . .

They were lucky. The dust was thick enough to take a track. Mutisya found where Kilatya had come on foot, walking from the Baboonery. That was easy. They fanned out from that point, working both sides of a circle.

It took them a long time. They studied every inch of the ground. They came up with three kinds of fresh tracks. One set of prints probably came from a jackal. They ignored that sign.

There were other tracks that were unmistakable. Royce had seen them a thousand times; they were one of the few tracks he could recognize on sight. They had been made by baboons. He could tell by the different sizes that there had been at least two of them.

The remaining tracks—if tracks they were—sent a chill down his spine. He had seen them only once before. Sharp-edged depressions, deep prints. Made by something heavy. As though a flat-bottomed post of hard wood or metal had been slammed into the earth. . . .

They found one other thing. A tuft of baboon hair caught in a thorny bush.

The evidence was clear. It was even possible to reconstruct what must have happened. Kilatya had been on guard at the Baboonery. Something had taken one of the baboons. Kilatya had followed that something into the bush. He had caught up with it here. And that had been the end of Kilatya.

It was clear, but it made no sense. Baboons did not kill human beings. They were capable of it, no doubt of that, but they just didn't *do* it. Certainly, one or two baboons would never attack a man. A whole troop might do it, although Royce had never heard of such a thing, but not a couple of animals on their own.

That left the other thing, the thing that made the deep prints. An elephant? The idea was absurd.

The facts were simple enough. The baboons and whatever had made those sharp-edged prints had come together here, just as they had at the Baboonery. Two baboons were missing. A baboon was dead, the body still in the freezer. And now Kilatya was dead.

Facts were fine, but facts alone were never enough. What did they mean? What *could* they mean?

The two men got back into the Land Rover and Royce drove the rough trail to the Baboonery. He took it easy, concerned for Kilatya's body. Whenever he hit a hole in the road the corpse thumped soddenly in the tarp.

It was afternoon when he reached the thatched buildings in the clearing. It was hot again despite the dark clouds blowing across the sky. The caged baboons coughed out a greeting. Royce stared at them, his hackles rising.

Welcome home, he thought.

The Baboonery seemed very small and very lonely and very isolated.

When the Land Rover stopped, there was a smell of fear and death in the air.

5

THERE WAS NO telephone at the Baboonery. There was no radio transmitter.

Royce told Kathy what had happened. He instructed Mutisya to stay with her and to make certain that the children did not stray from the main building. He climbed back into the Land Rover and made the short run to Matt Donaldson's safari camp—five neat green tents in a clearing located just before the trail crossed the Kikumbuliu. Matt's American clients were asleep in their tent, which simplified matters somewhat. Royce quickly explained the situation and Matt glanced at Kilatya's body.

"Get that bloke out of here, will you?" Donaldson said in a low voice. "You'll frighten my clients right out of their new safari boots."

"I'm taking him in to the police at Mitaboni."

"Want a bit of advice?"

Royce shrugged, wiping the sweat out of his eyes.

"Take old Kilatya out in the bush and plant him. Save

you all sorts of trouble. The local Sherlocks will swarm over this place like flies. They won't find out anything, you can bank on that. They'll muck up my safari and you'll be filling out forms until your arm drops off."

Royce shook his head. "Can't do that. You know the law. Dammit, a man has been *killed*. I've got to find out what the hell is going on."

"You won't find out from the police. In the old days, maybe. Not now. Royce, these people are forever killing one another. Or maybe it was an accident; I don't know. I say forget it. Get yourself another driver."

Royce felt a flash of anger. "It's not that simple. I'm taking him to Mitaboni. Will you look in on Kathy if I'm delayed?"

"Certainly. No offense, Royce. You do what you think best. It's your *shauri*. Just remember, I warned you. Now *please* get that body out of here before our friends emerge to sample the wonders of the African afternoon."

"Right. Thanks, Matt."

Royce turned the vehicle around, went back past the Baboonery, and headed toward the main road to Mitaboni. It was slow going and he could hear the tarp-wrapped body thumping behind him. When he finally emerged on the paved road he gunned the Land Rover with a sense of relief.

He still had a couple of daylight hours left when he got to Mitaboni. He pulled up in front of the ramshackle post office and got out into the sultry air. The flies began to settle on the tarp in the back of the Land Rover. He stepped into the public telephone booth outside the post office and closed the door. It took him half an hour to get a call through to the district headquarters at Machakos, a distance of a little better than one hundred miles. It took him another fifteen minutes to talk his way past a battery of officious clerks and get the ear of a captain in the Kenya Police. The captain told him that this was a very serious matter, which he already knew. The captain said that he was sure the local police could handle the situation, which Royce doubted. The captain thanked him for calling.

Royce left the telephone booth in something less than high good spirits. He was drenched with sweat. He drove across to the Mitaboni police station, carried Kilatya's body inside, and placed it on the long counter.

"I have a dead man here," he said to the building's only occupant.

The African policeman, dressed in a crisp blue shirt, shorts, and heavy shoes, thoughtfully unwrapped the tarp. "This man, he is dead."

"I know that."

"This matter is very serious."

"I know that."

"I will have to notify Machakos."

"I've done that."

The policeman eyed him suspiciously. "We will see."

Royce sighed and sat down. He stared at the fly-covered body on the counter while the officer attempted to contact Machakos. Another forty minutes went by. The policeman returned from his labors and confronted Royce. "I am in charge. This is a very serious matter. There must be an investigation."

"Good. That's why I'm here."

It took Royce two hours to relate what had happened while the policeman took laborious notes. The body remained on the counter the entire time. Nobody came into the station and nobody left it. The policeman informed Royce that he would be out the next day to search for "clues." Royce thanked him and left.

Darkness had fallen and the air was cooler. Stars gleamed through the broken clouds. Royce was tired, hungry, and disgusted. He made a quick detour on the way home to tell Bob Russell what had happened. He refused Russell's offer of food and pushed on to the Baboonery.

It was late when he got there. All the lights were on and Mutisya was sitting on the front steps.

"Everything okay, Mutisya?"

"Okay, Mr. Royce."

"Thank you. Go and get some sleep, Mutisya. Tell Elijah to post a watch."

Royce went on inside. He was too tired to think,
He knew one thing.
Everything was definitely *not* okay.

The police arrived the next morning—all three of them, comprising the entire Mitaboni police detachment. They proceeded to launch their investigation, and they soon had the place in a state of total confusion.

Royce held himself under control; there was nothing else he could do. The scene before him was something between a Marx Brothers' movie and watching a man trying to empty the ocean with a bucket. The police checked everything they could think of, including driver's licenses, passports, and trapping permits. They examined the dead baboon in the freezer. They grilled the African staff. They studied the baboons in the cages. They marched down to Donaldson's camp and looked at the tents. After a two-hour break for lunch—cooked by Wathome—they actually had Royce drive them out to where Kilatya's body had been found. They studied the tracks and scribbled away in notebooks.

When they were all through they went into a huddle. The officer in charge called Royce to him.

"This matter is very serious," he said.

Royce couldn't think of anything to say to that.

"You will not be charged," he said.

Royce couldn't think of anything to say to that either.

"It is our decision," the policeman said solemnly, "that this man was killed by baboons unknown."

Royce bit down hard on his pipe. He had the distinct feeling that wild laughter would not be appreciated.

"Wild animals in cages are very dangerous. Be more careful in times to come. If there is more trouble we will have to think again about the matter of trapping permits."

The policeman saluted and took his leave.

Royce watched the police Land Rover disappear in a cloud of dust. He put his hands on his hips. "Well, I'll be damned," he said.

He went into the kitchen and got a bottle of beer. He needed it.

He sprawled on the uncomfortable leather-covered

couch, waiting for dinner, staring at nothing. Kathy was busy with the kids back in the bedroom, which was just as well. He didn't feel much like talking.

Somehow, he had to organize his thoughts.

The police had been a waste of time, but he couldn't blame them. This thing was completely outside the range of their experience. They knew their business when it came to accidents on the Mombasa road or cattle rustling or witch killings. but this . . .

A sound in the sky. A baboon torn apart with superhuman strength. Mysterious tracks. A man killed trailing a baboon. . . .

Was there a cop in the world who could have made any sense out of all that?

Royce himself did not know what to think. The comic-opera interlude had done nothing to ease his mind. He knew that he was in danger even if he did not know exactly what the danger was. He was isolated here, vulnerable. He had a wife and two children to consider.

He also had a shipment of baboons to get out. He had men to feed and pay, equipment for which he was responsible. He could not just lock the door and walk out.

He fired up his pipe. His mind kept wandering. It was all so strange, so strange that he was here at all. . . .

Two years ago, Africa had been little more than a splotch on a map to Royce Crawford. It was halfway between Edgar Rice Burroughs and actors shooting lions on TV—lions that were invariably "man-eaters terrorizing the native villages."

Royce had settled into a comfortable rut. It was a more interesting rut than most and he might have remained in it for the rest of his life if it had not been for Ben Wallace. After Royce had graduated from the University of Texas and served his time in the army, he was too restless to spend his years parked in an office by day and stuck in a tract house by night. There were two things that Royce liked. He enjoyed hunting and fishing, which kept him outdoors, and he liked to write straightforward prose that bore some relationship to the English language. In both of these activities, he was terribly old-fashioned. His country had become an urban land; most Texans lived in cities now, and their most violent form of exercise consisted of carrying beer from the refrigerator to the backyard barbecue pit. The writing that was currently much admired seemed to deal exclusively with sex hang-ups and the feeble joys of drug addiction.

Royce made the happy discovery that there was a market for more or less factual stories about hunting and fishing. He taught himself to take passable photographs, and he made an unspectacular living writing for magazines like *Field and Stream* and *Outdoor Life.* It was fun, but it got tougher as time went on. There were only so many basic variants on how to fish for bass in stock ponds and how to pot Texas deer in the wilds of Kerr County. He had to keep on the move, looking for unusual ideas, and living began to get complicated.

Then Ben Wallace had called.

Royce went to Houston to talk to him. He knew in a rough kind of way about the Foundation's medical research work in Africa, and he figured that Wallace wanted him to do an article on baboons. Instead, Wallace offered him a job in Africa.

"Why me?" Royce asked. "I'm not a doctor. I don't know anything about Africa."

"We don't want a doctor," Ben Wallace said. "*You* are not going to experiment on the baboons. We fly doctors in sometimes for work on the spot, but mostly we are concerned with getting the baboons out to the doctors—it's more economical that way. We want a man who knows something about animals. You do. We want a man who can hunt for meat. You can. We want a man who can get along in somewhat primitive circumstances. You do that all the time. We want a man who can get along with people. We think you can. We want a man with some education. Your college record was a good one. Don't sell yourself short, Mr. Crawford."

"Okay. I'm the answer to the Foundation's prayer. Why is the Foundation the answer to mine?"

Ben Wallace smiled. "May I speak frankly?"

"This would seem to be the time for it, Dr. Wallace."

"Very well. I've checked you out very carefully indeed. You're making a living out of your writing and that's about all. You don't have any compelling ties to keep you here for the next few years. Your oldest daughter—Susan— will be starting to school, but your wife can teach her the first-grade stuff. Susan will get far more out of a year or two in Africa than she's likely to get around here. You *could* go."

"Maybe I could. Why should I?"

"Look at it this way. We'll pay you ten thousand dollars a year to manage the Baboonery. That's about what you make in a good year here. The thing is, almost all of that will be clear profit. You will have no living expenses. We'll pay your passage over and back. Your quarters will be provided, and your food and a reasonable liquor allowance. We'll supply the ammunition for your hunting. Your job won't take more than five or six hours a day. You'll be sitting right smack in the middle of some of the best game country left in the world. You can do plenty of hunting and take all the pictures you need. You should be able to sell as many stories from there as you could poking around shooting jack rabbits in Texas. You can even take some time off and go fishing—there are some fine trout streams on Mount Kenya, you know, and there is good Indian Ocean fishing at Malindi. You'll have some interesting years at the Baboonery, and you'll wind up with two or three times the money you could make if you stayed home. That's why you should go. If you've got any arguments against that, I'd like to hear them."

Royce hadn't been able to think of any arguments.

That was how he had wound up at the Baboonery.

Of course, Ben Wallace had left a few things out of his description of paradise. Little things like fear and isolation and death. . . .

Royce refilled his pipe. Houston seemed more than a world away.

Perhaps Kilatya *had* been killed by a baboon—or by baboons—unknown. Except that *unknown* was the wrong word. The right word was *alien*. Face it. Something had come down out of the sky. Something was walking through the bush that left an unearthly track. Something was *changing* the baboons. . . .

How? Why?

Royce did not know and could not know. But even if his imagination was playing tricks on him, one thing was obvious: he ought to get Kathy and the kids away from the Baboonery. He could take them to Nairobi, put them up in a hotel whether they wanted to go or not. Then he could come back alone. Find out for sure what in the hell was going on. Then make a final decision. . . .

Wathome stuck his head in from the kitchen and announced that dinner was ready. Kathy came in with Barbara.

"Where's Susan?"

"She's not feeling well. I don't know what's wrong with her. I put her to bed; she says she doesn't want any dinner." Kathy looked worried.

Royce joined them at the table. "Well, let's eat our dinner anyway. Maybe we'll all feel better later."

He hardly tasted his food. Kathy seemed so distracted that he did not try to talk to her. Perhaps it would be more sensible to wait until Susan was over her cold or whatever it was. He had a lot of work to do. As long as Matt Donaldson was camped down the road they were not alone.

Better to wait. . . .

After the dinner dishes had been cleared away and

Wathome had gone, the night seemed suddenly very large and very still. The moon, like a coin of old silver, was high in a cloud-shrouded sky. The air was chilly and a small breeze stirred through the leaves of the banana trees. The baboons were restless, coughing and grunting in their cages. Somewhere, far away in the depths of the night, a solitary leopard gave a harsh cry of anger at a missed kill.

Royce sat on the edge of the bed, puffing on hs pipe. "Hear that *chui?* I know just how that old leopard feels. I thought we might get someplace with the police in here, but we're right where we were before. I really think we ought to get you and the kids to Nairobi. A couple of weeks at the Norfolk would do you good."

Kathy took off her dress and hung it in the closet. She went over to check on Susan and then sat down next to Royce, smoothing her slip over over her knees. "Let's wait until Susan is better. She feels hot to me. Then we'll talk about it."

Royce kissed her, gently at first.

"Sex fiend," she whispered. "You might at least turn the light out."

"I was just being friendly."

"Be a little less friendly. But put that stinking pipe away. I have to draw the line somewhere."

Royce got up, turned off the light, undressed, and went to his wife.

Later, when he thought Kathy had gone to sleep, he got up again and pulled on his clothes.

"Where are you going?"

He bent over and kissed her lightly. "Just going to have a look around. I won't be long. Go back to sleep."

"Be careful," she said drowsily. "I love you."

"I love you," he said quietly. *Lord,* he thought, *I really do. I'm an anachronism. If anything ever happens to her or the kids . . .*

He picked up his pipe and the long flashlight he kept on the dresser. Closing the door behind him, he took the rifle out of the gun safe and checked its load. He went into the sitting room, filled his pipe, and lit it. It was bitter with too much smoking.

He did not turn on any lights.

He stepped outside, closing the door softly behind him. He could see fairly well by the light of the moon and stars. It was a strange world, a world without colors, but it was not difficult to orient himself. Objects had sharp outlines in the night; everything was either a luminous gray or a jet black, with nothing in between. It was almost cold. He wished that he had worn a jacket.

He started walking, circling the buildings, not using his flashlight. He was challenged once by Nzioki, one of Elijah's men. He was faintly surprised to find that the watch was actually being kept. He identified himself and kept walking. He was not looking for anything in particular. He was just looking.

At the very least, he could prowl around and satisfy himself that there was nothing lurking under the bedroom window. *I'm like an old maid checking under the bed,* he thought. *What do I do if I find someone—or something?*

He went all the way around the main building. He

saw nothing unusual and heard nothing. He repeated his effort on the building that housed the operating rooms and his office. Nothing there.

He stood for a long time and watched the quarters of the African staff. There were no lights showing. Everything was quiet. He walked along the line of baboon cages, not getting too close. The animals stirred and grunted sleepily. That was all.

Royce knocked out his pipe against his shoe, refilled it from the tin he had put in his hip pocket, and lit it with a match. The flare of the light seemed very bright. It took his eyes a long moment to adjust again after the match went out.

Little man, what now?

He started off along the dirt road that eventually skirted the railroad track. This was the way that Kilatya had gone. He walked almost silently, flashlight in his left hand and rifle in his right. He did not intend to go far. Once he left the cleared area of the Baboonery and the smell of man, there was always the chance of running into animals. He did not fancy running into a big cat in the middle of the night, with or without a rifle. He smiled a little, remembering those ads that filled the magazines he wrote for. *Attacked by a killer lion, I would have been lost without my Little Dandy Hotshot Flashlight Batteries! Blinding the beast with my flashlight's titanic glare, I whipped out my pipe and blew smoke in his nose until he fell to the earth. . . .*

The whistle of an oncoming train startled him for a moment. The thing always took him by surprise, although it was a soft whistle, the sort of sound he always associated with a model railroad. A train just seemed so unlikely here.

It was even quieter once the train had gone by. There wasn't a sound in the bush. It was a land of the dead.

He was ready to turn back when something caught his eye. Off there in the distance to his right. At first, he thought it was a light from the train. But the light did not move and the *quality* of it was wrong. It was a soft, pale glow, almost like moonlight. It was steady and utterly silent.

Royce took a deep breath. That glow was coming from the area where that thing from the sky had come down. It couldn't be more than a couple of miles away.

He did not pause to consider a plan of action. He wanted to get a look at whatever was producing that eerie light. He headed toward it.

There was no trail. He walked directly into the bush, moving as quietly as possible, using his flashlight sparingly. The glow ahead of him seemed to intensify that darkness. Thorns ripped at his clothing. Twice he had to backtrack to get around thick clumps of brush. He was worried about snakes. Nesting birds fluttered up before him. His hands were wet with sweat in the cool night air.

The glow was a little closer. He figured he had covered half a mile, maybe more.

Then, quite suddenly, the glow . . . stopped.

It wasn't there.

There was only the moonlight and the stars and the hush of the night.

Royce stood stock still and waited. Long minutes crept by. The glow did not return.

He finally turned and began to retrace his steps. There was nothing else to do. Without the light to guide him it was madness to search the bush in the middle of the night. He made his way back to the trail and almost ran toward the dark Baboonery.

He was very tired but his mind was churning. He went into the cold kitchen and drank a bottle of beer, standing at the window and looking out at the cloud-shadowed stars. The beer helped a little.

He walked silently into the bedroom and checked his sleeping family. He put the rifle under the bed. He undressed in the dark and slipped into bed next to Kathy. She stirred but did not awaken.

Royce lay in the silence staring at nothing. His mind was filled with questions that had no answers.

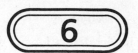

THE DAYS DRIFTED by, one by one. Royce was not lulled by the routine of running the Baboonery, but he was preoccupied. He had a lot to do, and he made the mistake of postponing the decisions he had to make.

Each day the dark clouds rolled through the great sky, throwing racing shadows across the parched land. It was hot again, hotter than ever with a dry wind that picked at the naked trees and piled the red dust in gritty drifts that rippled like sand dunes. The animals were pink-eyed and irritable, sticking close to the lowering streams. The white termite hills, taller than a man, stood out like sentinels in the barren plains. The promise of rain was worse than the blue skies and blazing sun had been; day after day the arid earth stared up at the tantalizing swollen clouds, waiting, waiting, forever waiting. . . .

Susan seemed to be getting better, but she had a lingering fever. Her temperature shot up briefly to 102, then dropped down to around 99 and stayed there. She rested comfortably; she slept a lot and was very quiet. At least she was not getting worse. Royce was afraid to take her to Nairobi until she recovered some of her strength.

Kathy doctored Susan from the suitcase full of medical supplies she had insisted on bringing with her. She stayed with her day and night, and Susan was pleased with all the attention. Barbara was left to young Mbali, the shamba boy, which suited her fine. Royce was amazed at the patience shown by Mbali, who was little more than a child himself. Barbara adored him. Every night she would tell Royce with shining eyes of some wonderful new thing that "Bally" had done with her. Royce was deeply grateful to Mbali, and told him so. Mbali just smiled, looking down at his bare feet, and shyly said that he liked the girls. He said that he prayed for Susan at night, and Royce believed him.

Royce made no further attempt to search the bush. It was too much like asking for trouble. He did not see the strange glow in the night again.

They built strong wooden shipping crates for the baboons. The generator broke down and Royce spent a day repairing it. Royce and Mutisya found a good new area for the traps and salted it with maize and pineapple to bring in the baboons. They went out with a crew of men and finished the dirty job of moving the heavy traps.

The trapping went slowly, and Royce needed some big males for his shipment. It seemed to him that the ratio of trapped males to females was unusually low. There were a lot of empty traps. He examined them carefully. Sometimes, the bait was gone but nothing was caught in the trap. Baboons did escape from the traps occasionally, but he could find no sign that the traps had been forced from within. If something were releasing baboons from the traps, then that something had learned to open the traps properly. There were no damaged traps. At the Baboonery, the cages were undisturbed.

Royce saw baboons lurking at the edge of the clearing around the Baboonery several times. It had happened before; even elephants had been known to parade along the trail right by the front door. The baboons bothered him now, though. They seemed to be *watching* him. He knew that he was jittery but he saw no point in taking chances. Whenever he spotted baboons near the clearing he took his light rifle and drilled them neatly through the head. The buzzards did the rest.

The day finally came when Matt Donaldson loaded his clients into his Land Rover and carted them back to Nairobi to catch a plane for home. Matt left his camp intact, explaining that he intended to return shortly with some new hunters he was expecting.

Royce's sense of uneasiness increased sharply when Matt had gone. He was afraid to make his trapping run and leave Kathy and the kids alone. Susan was definitely getting better. She was stronger now, almost her old self again. Surely, the trip to Nairobi would not harm her in a day or two. . . .

He decided to tell Kathy to pack her gear.

He stood on the steps of the Baboonery, staring up at the cloud-darkened sky. He felt as though he were trapped in a dream, marking time.

The hot, dry wind plucked at his shirt.
If only it would rain, he thought crazily.
If only it would rain.

Royce woke up early in the morning on the first day of November. He was fully awake but he did not move for a moment. Kathy had been up during the night with Susan and she was still sound asleep. He looked at the white curtains on the windows. They were hardly moving at all; the air was still. He could see the light of the sun behind the curtains.

The cloud cover was breaking, then. The rains were already late. Some years, he knew, the rains never came. . . .

There was a curious heavy smell in the air. Royce couldn't quite place it. He got up quietly, pulled on his clothes, and went into the empty kitchen. He took out the electric coffeepot that Wathome never used and plugged it in.

He stepped outside to have a look around.

He saw him at once, sitting under his bedroom window. A big male baboon. The animal just sat there, staring at him. Its red-rimmed eyes were challenging and unafraid. There was white saliva on his snout.

Royce felt a stab of fear. For a moment, he could not move. He had seen plenty of baboons in his time, but this one was . . . different. There was a cold intelligence looking out through those animal eyes. The beast was *studying* him.

"Okay, Big Daddy," Royce whispered. "You just sit there for ten more seconds."

Royce whirled and started back inside to get his rifle. He stopped before he got through the door. That smell. It was much stronger now. The baboon, yes, but there was something else.

The baboon still made no move.

Royce looked down the trail that led to the main road.

The fear came again, a fear that was close to horror.

He ran into the house, trying to think, trying not to panic.

It would take more than a rifle to help him now.

Royce hesitated for a long minute in the kitchen. It would not help matters any to go flying off in all directions at once. He had to get things organized, and he had to do it fast. His senses were suddenly sharp: he was aware of the coffeepot bubbling on the table, the hum of the refrigerator, the nervous stirring of the baboons outside in their cages. . . .

He strode quickly into the breezeway between the kitchen and the bedroom and opened the gun safe. He took out the .375 and a box of cartridges.

He went into the bedroom and bent over his sleeping wife. He touched her shoulder, gently.

"Kathy. Kathy, wake up."

She stirred and opened sleep-fogged eyes.

"Kathy honey. Come on, wake up. We've got trouble. I need your help."

She sat up, coming back to consciousness with a visible effort. "What is it? Is Susan . . . ?"

"Susan's okay. She's still asleep. Are you awake enough to remember what I tell you? I haven't got much time."

Kathy rubbed her eyes. "I guess so. What's going on?"

"Come over here to the window." Royce kept his voice steady.

She climbed out of bed and followed him to the window. He pulled back the curtains. The baboon was gone, but that was a minor problem now. He pointed. "Look at that."

Already, it was worse. Away across the red-brown earth, not over four hundred yards from the Baboonery buildings, a wall of dirty smoke boiled up into the morning sky. A jagged line of orange flame blazed under the smoke. It was a big fire, a very big fire, and even as they watched it seemed to move closer. A kudu bolted out of the bush, ran across the clearing, and vanished behind the main building. The sky was full of birds.

"Jesus H. Christ," Kathy said.

"Get the picture? Just another humdrum episode of *Breakfast with the Crawfords.*"

Kathy managed a smile and Royce found himself smiling in return. Kathy had a strength in her that always surprised him. Whatever his problems, she wasn't one of them. "Okay," he said. "You get the kids up, take them into the kitchen, and give them something to eat. There's time for that. Make sure Susan gets her medicine. There's coffee ready in the pot. Take the .38 with you and keep it with you—it's in the dresser. When you finish in the kitchen, you and the kids go and sit in the Land Rover. I want to know exactly where you are. If we can't lick this fire—and our chances are not too bright—we'll take off down that back road to Mitaboni. How was Susan last night?"

"About the same. When you called me I was afraid. . ."

"I'm scared right now, I'll tell you that. Dammit, Kathy, something is trying to burn me out of here."

"Maybe you ought to take the hint."

Royce realized with a kind of wonder that he hadn't really considered quitting, not yet. Getting Kathy and the children out was one thing, running him off was something else again. "If I'm licked, that'll be the time to run away. I'm not licked yet."

She didn't argue. "We're wasting time. Do what you have to do. But for God's sake be careful. I'm not ready to be a widow yet."

Royce grabbed the .375 and ran out the back door of the breezeway. The sharp smell of the fire was stronger now. The baboons in the cages were pacing and grunting. Behind him, the great cloud of smoke rose like a seething brown mountain into the still air.

He had time for some fleeting thoughts even as he ran; all of his senses had speeded up to the point that he could look back on his usual self as though he had been a slow-motion zombie. A man never realized how much he took for granted until it was all taken away. In the world Royce had known, when someone in your family got sick, you called the doctor. If someone threatened your life, you called the police. If fire broke out, you picked up the phone and hollered for the fire department.

It was different here, worlds and centuries different. He began to appreciate what a people like the Kamba were up against. Plagues, famines, fires—what could a man do? A fire in a dry land was not just an annoyance, not just an insurance-covered curiosity staged as a passing entertainment—it was a blazing monster, an all-devouring horror, an implacable wall of destruction.

It was a killer, and his weapons against it were a joke. And if the baboons turned on them . . .

"Elijah!" he hollered, beating on the door of his headman's quarters. "Mutisya! Wathome! Come out quick, hurry! *Moto!* Fire!"

He waited impatiently as the men tumbled out. He did have water; that was something. But the pressure was nothing much, and he had only the one hose that Mbali used for watering the garden and keeping the dust down. He couldn't stop that fire with a garden hose, that was for sure. He had shovels and axes and rakes, but he didn't have enough manpower. . . .

And he didn't know enough, either. He had never fought a big fire in his life.

Well, this was a good time to start learning.

The Africans stared at the smoke and sniffed the air. They did not panic. They simply waited for instructions. Their confidence in him was touching but not very helpful.

"Elijah. What should we do?"

Elijah examined the smoke solemnly through his tinted glasses. "It is a very large fire, Mr. Royce."

Royce waited. Elijah said nothing else.

"In the place where the doctors cut on the baboons," Mutisya volunteered, "there is a machine for putting out fires."

Royce had forgotten about the fire extinguisher—not that it made any difference. One fire extinguisher for a forest fire—it might have been funny under other circumstances. It wasn't particularly hilarious now.

"Okay," he said. "This is what we'll do. Mbali, you take the hose and put the water on everything you can reach. Try to get the thatch on top of the buildings as wet as you can. Do you understand?"

"*Ndio.*" The boy, pleased to be trusted with important work, ran off to get the hose.

"Elijah, take all of the men and supply them with tools—shovels, rakes, axes, pangas if you've got some. Get between the fire and the buildings and clear that area of anything that will burn. Then we'll try to dig some kind of a trench—at least get the grass turned under. I'll go down to Donaldson's camp and round up the men there. I'll join you as soon as I can. Any questions?"

Elijah shook his head. He looked dubious. "It is a very large fire, Mr. Royce," he said again.

"Do your best. That's all I ask. I'll be back in a minute."

Royce didn't wait to check up on them. There was no time. He piled into the Land Rover—Kathy and the kids

were still inside the building—and jolted down to Donaldson's camp. He found four men there and some good tools.
He drove them back to the Baboonery, parked the Land
Rover in a reasonably shady spot for Kathy, and ran for the
fire.

As soon as he got close to it his heart sank. The fire
was an inferno—a solid wall of blistering heat and choking
smoke. It was moving, not fast but inexorably, toward the
Baboonery. It was a noisy fire: it hissed and crackled and
roared at him, telling him things he did not want to know.

He had a couple of things in his favor, he figured. He
tried to concentrate on them. There was no wind at all.
That was a real break. Once that fire got a wind behind it
they were through. And they had kept the land around the
buildings fairly clear of brush; there wasn't much to burn
in this area. If they could keep the flames from jumping to
the buildings . . .

Don't think. Work, dammit. Set an example.

He uprooted small, dry bushes and ran with them
away from the fire. He scooped up sticks and twigs and
tufts of brown grass. The sweat poured from his body in
drops and trickles and streams. Smoke reddened his eyes
and clogged his throat. The fire roared at him, punched at
him with fists of heat. He lost all track of time; he was
trapped in an eternal *now*, a moment that stretched on
forever, a moment where nothing changed, nothing made
any difference. . . .

He ran back and Mbali hosed down his hot skin with
water. Even the water felt hot. He went on working in a
kind of madness, his eyes wild and bloodshot.

The fire drove them back. They couldn't get close to the flames; the searing heat reached out for them, hammered them with a wind from hell. Mutisya's hair began to smolder and he ran screaming for the hose, beating at his head with his raw and bleeding hands.

There were snakes, too many snakes, driven from cover by the crackling heat. Royce saw a six-foot green mamba, its thin body writhing in agony in the dirt. He reached for his rifle, picked it up, and tried to take aim. His hands were shaking so badly he couldn't draw a bead on the snake. Wathome ran up and sliced off its head with a panga.

They were losing their fight. Dimly, Royce knew that they could not win. The fire was too big, too fierce, too totally overpowering.

One more effort. . . .

"Stop!" he yelled. No one heard him. "Stop!" he screamed at the top of his voice. "The trench! Dig the trench!"

He grabbed a shovel and retreated away from the heat. The smoke was so thick he could hardly catch his breath. He began to dig, trying to make a wide furrow the fire could not jump. The crust of the earth was as hard as rock. He jammed the shovel into it, cursing it, fighting it. The handle of the shovel was slippery with his own blood. He was so weak that his knees were trembling. His mind began to spin.

He sensed an animal running by him. Heard the thuds of hooves on the unyielding ground. Saw stripes. A zebra. . . .

He fell. He could not get up. He started to crawl away from the fire. His throat was a parched ache. He could not swallow.

He had failed. They had to get out before they were all killed.

"Give it up!" he tried to yell. His voice was little more than a croak. "Get the lorry, get the men out. Elijah . . ."

Then he heard it. He heard it before he felt anything at all. A hissing sound, a strange hissing, a new hissing that cut through the roar of the fire.

It sounded . . .

What did it sound like?

He shook his head. It was like a campfire when you poured what was left of the coffee on it. A wet hissing, a hissing like water on flame. . . .

He rolled over, turning his face up to the sky.

He felt it then. Water. Big fat drops of water. Rain!

He said it aloud, tasting the word, tasting the cool drops that splashed on his parched lips. "Rain, rain, rain. . . ."

It came down harder, dripping through the dense clouds of smoke.

He threw out his arms and let it come.

It poured. It rained buckets and lakes and rivers. It soaked him. His skin drank it in like a blotter.

He began to laugh.

He laughed like a crazy man, letting the rain pound him into a growing sea of mud.

Suddenly, incredibly, the whole world was laughing.

He pulled himself to his feet, grabbed his rifle, and

staggered for shelter. He couldn't stop laughing. He didn't want to stop. Everyone was laughing.

Rain!

"Come on, rain!" he muttered. "Don't quit. Don't ever quit. Rain like you've never rained before!"

He jerked open the breezeway door and stepped inside. He stood there, swaying. Kathy had come in and she stared at him almost without recognition. His clothes were torn, his hair singed. His face was black and greasy with smoke. His arms were smeared with blood and dirt.

"It's raining," he said inanely.

Then he collapsed in a heap on the floor.

When he came to, he could hear it before he opened his eyes. A wild wet drumming on the roof. He could smell it. A fresh clean damp smell, the sweet smell of water, a smell of oceans of rain pouring down on a thirsty earth.

Royce knew the thrill of rain in a dry land. He was no stranger to the electric excitement of a cloudburst after long months of dry, searing heat. But he had never felt it this keenly before. This was more than rain. This was . . .

Well, hell.

This was life itself.

He opened his eyes.

"The fire?" His voice was a painful rasp.

Kathy handed him a glass of water. He choked it down. It was cool on his throat, cool and wet and soothing.

"There isn't any fire. There's nothing out there but a puddle as big as the Indian Ocean."

Royce tried to get out of bed, failed, and tried again. This time he made it. His body was one dull ache from head to toe. He stumbled over to the window and looked out.

It was a new world. The earth was gray under leaden skies that poured down silvery sheets of rain. Where the fire had been there was an ugly carbon-black scar. The naked land around the Baboonery was splashed with miniature lakes. Rain beat a tattoo on the roof and dripped in a steady stream from the thatch. In the puddles, the big drops hit like bullets, throwing up little geysers of spray. A wet smell filled the air with a heavy, tangible scent.

He took a deep breath. "What time is it?"

"About eight in the morning. You've been out for around fourteen hours. I figured you could use the sleep."

"Where did it come from?"

"It started to cloud up around noon yesterday. I guess you didn't see it because of the smoke. At first I didn't think anything of it—we've had the clouds before—and then I couldn't get through to you. You were . . . well, I've never seen you like that before."

"I hope you never see me that way again. Did you catch the news last night?"

She nodded. "The rains have started all over southern Kenya. It was raining in Nairobi when the news came on. I guess this is it."

Royce sat down on the bed again. He felt like hell. Everything hit him with a rush. He'd seen that crazy

baboon and something had tried to burn them out of the
Baboonery, and he had cleverly passed out and left his wife
alone. If anything had happened . . .

"The kids?"

"They're having breakfast with Wathome."

"Susan?"

"She's better, I think. Maybe this rain has helped her,
somehow. There was no fever this morning." She sat down
next to him and took his hand. "Stop worrying. You're in
no shape to wrestle with any problems yet. We're all safe
and the fire is out."

"But : . ."

"After breakfast, okay? You didn't get around to eating
yesterday—it's not like you to forget *that.*"

"I don't have time to eat. . . .

"Royce. Look at me. If you get sick and conk out on
us, what happens then? You go take a shower—the water's
a little muddy but not too bad yet—and get some clean
clothes on. I'll fix breakfast. *Then* we'll worry. Deal?"

"Deal."

Royce peeled off his pajamas—Kathy had somehow
managed to get his dirty clothes off after he had passed
out—and stepped gingerly into the shower stall. He turned
on the taps and waited. The water got lukewarm but not
hot. Maybe that was just as well; there never was any really
hot water until the cook stove had been going for two or
three hours. The water was brownish and gritty but it felt
good against his skin. He let it soak in for ten minutes or
so and then shaved and dressed. He felt better. His hands
were cut and blistered and his hair and eyebrows were

singed, but otherwise he seemed to be okay except for a persistent ache in his shoulders.

He had been lucky, very lucky. But it would not do to push his luck too far. He had been warned. The fates would not likely intervene on his behalf again. He had to get Kathy and the kids away from this place.

He stepped out of the bedroom into the breezeway. The rain was coming down in solid sheets and the plank floor was slick with moisture. The dry warmth of the kitchen was suddenly very welcome.

He shook hands with Wathome and thanked him for all he had done the day before. Then he greeted the kids. Barby was bright-eyed as usual, and eager to go play in the rain. Susan looked better, much better. He gave her a kiss. Surely, she could stand the trip to Nairobi now.

He seated himself at the wooden dining table in the main room and discovered that he was famished. He put away a pile of Kathy's scrambled eggs and six slices of fried Spam—available at the curiously named Supermarket in Nairobi, an edifice that contained everything from groceries to a tearoom, and an institution that endeared itself to visitors by stocking such exotic foods as hamburger and Chef Boy-Ar-Dee spaghetti. As far as Royce was concerned, Spam was considerably better than Kenya bacon, and it hit the spot this morning. He drank three cups of coffee and began to feel almost human.

He pushed his cup back. "There," he said. "Now we can attend to our worrying."

"Okay." Kathy lit a cigarette. She looked fresh and

relaxed, as though she had been enjoying herself on a carefree vacation. "Worry away."

Royce considered. "I'm not much for giving orders," he said slowly, "but I'm giving one now. It's time for you and the kids to get out of here. Susan is well enough to take the trip to Nairobi. We can put you up at the Norfolk. I can come back here and do what has to be done. I can take care of myself, but it's too dangerous for you to hang around here. I . . . what the devil are you laughing about?"

Kathy's laughter had an edge of hysteria to it; she wasn't as relaxed as she looked. "I listened to the news while you were taking your shower. I'm afraid your plan won't work."

"Why the hell not?"

"You hear that rain out there?"

"I'm not deaf."

"Well, old sport, we've had better than six inches of rain since yesterday. There's no end to it in sight, either. We could never make it through that gunk to the main road. Even if we *did* make it we couldn't go anywhere."

Royce felt a sudden cold knot in the pit of his stomach. He hadn't been thinking. This was Kenya, not the United States. The main road to Nairobi was paved after a fashion, but the bridges . . .

"There are cars stuck all along the road," Kathy said. "Every last crossing between here and Nairobi is under water, and it's the same way between here and Mombasa."

"The train?"

"They're holding them at both ends of the line. Same deal—tracks covered with water and a couple of the bridges too dangerous to cross."

Royce stood up. "That's just great."

He listened to the rain pounding down on the thatch roof. He should have known. Everything stopped when the rains came. Even back home, all through the southwest, a good gully-washer could knock out a road. And here . . .

"How are we fixed for food?"

"Pretty good. Enough for a couple of weeks, anyway."

Royce pulled at his ear. He had plenty of petrol on hand; he could keep the generator and the pumps going for a month if he didn't use the truck or the Land Rover. And he wouldn't be using the vehicles in that soup out there. They were in no immediate danger from the rain. Unhappily, the rain was the least of his worries.

"We'll just have to wait until the water goes down," he said, trying to get a confidence into his voice that he was far from feeling. Kathy had had enough shocks. She wasn't Superwoman. He had to be careful, very careful. "It can't keep on raining like this for long. It doesn't rain *continuously* during the rainy season. If the sun comes out for a day or two we'll be able to make it."

"If the bridges hold."

"We'll worry about crossing the bridges when we can get to them, to coin a phrase. I'd better go out and check things over. We may have a flood on our hands if this keeps up."

"Royce?"

He knew what was coming. He did not know what he could say. He waited.

"Royce, what *is* it? I mean . . . what's happening? Is there something *after* us?" Kathy laughed nervously, almost in embarrassment. There had been no melodrama in the world she knew. They had all been conditioned to a different kind of life. Indian raids, ghosts, outbreaks of plague—those things were over and done with, dead as the dinosaurs. Even here, linked by an umbilical cord to the world outside, such things were anachronisms. They just couldn't happen. The fabric of their lives, the assumptions they took for granted—they could not simply *disappear.*

Royce hesitated. The words were hard to say. There was a kind of magic to words. If you did not put a name to a thing, it was not quite real. It might go away, it might be nothing at all. . . .

Say it. Spit it out. She has a right to know.

"It's just a guess, Kathy," he said. "I may be wrong. I hope I'm wrong. But I think we have visitors. And I don't think they come from . . . well, anywhere on this earth."

She stared at him. She seemed shocked not so much by what he said as the fact that *he* had said it. "You? Things from another world? You always said those people—people who believed in that stuff—you always said they were a bunch of nuts."

He shrugged. "I said I'd believe it when I saw it with my own eyes. I think I have. I don't give a damn about theories. I don't care if a million lunatics saw visions in their backyards. All I know is that I'm faced with a situation and I have to deal with it as best I can. I can't refuse to face it just because of some stupid name tags. Call that thing I saw a glotz if you want to. I think we've got one."

"But here? In the middle of nowhere? It's crazy. What would they want here?"

"Facts aren't crazy just because we don't happen to understand them. Let's assume they want baboons, for openers. That's what they've taken. Let's assume they want us. We're the ones who are here—you and I and the kids and Wathome and Mutisya and Elijah and the rest."

"But *why*? It doesn't make any sense."

"It doesn't make any sense to *us*. Why should it? If there really are beings out there somewhere, and if they did decide to pay us a call, their motives might be absolutely alien to us. Maybe they came all this way to do the equivalent of throwing a pie in our face. Maybe they came here because they have a passion for snails or butterflies or baobab trees—how in the hell would I know?"

Kathy, strangely, looked relieved. The unknown was a fearful thing. But this sort of notion—something that rational people had laughed at for years—this couldn't be *serious*. "This will all seem funny in a day or two. There must be some perfectly reasonable explanation for it all. The fire could have started naturally—a spark from the train, an African tossing a cigarette into the bush. Maybe the baboons are just sick or something."

"Maybe." Royce managed a smile. "Maybe I'm just tired. But it *is* raining, and I've got work to do."

He walked into the bedroom to get his raincoat and boots. The rain was coming down in buckets. There was half an inch of water on the floor of the breezeway.

He listened to the rains with new ears. The rains had saved the Baboonery, no doubt of that. Probably, the rains had saved his neck as well. But there was a bitter irony in those driving rains.

They were completely isolated now. There could be no help from anyone. The rains could not alter the basic fact: someone—something—was out to get them. He did not believe for a moment that there was no logic or reason to *their* actions, whoever or whatever *they* might be. He was ready to take them at face value. They had come. They had taken baboons. They had killed. They had threatened the Baboonery.

And here he was, with his family.

Sitting ducks.

He was cut off as surely as though he had been trapped on the moon.

7

ROYCE STUCK THE .38 in his jacket pocket where it would stay dry and stepped outside. It was incredible how much everything had changed. The very air had a new smell to it, an underwater smell, a smell of sand on the beach when the tide ran out. His boots sank into gummy mud that was inches thick. There was a solid sheet of water beginning only thirty yards or so back of the baboon cages. The gray sky was thick and close and the rain poured down with numbing force.

He stood in the driving rain and tried to think. It was at least possible that the beings who had come out of the sky might be slowed up in their activities by the rain. It was also possible that they might welcome it; he could not know. In any event, there were three things that had to be done without delay.

He slogged around to the men's quarters and rapped on Elijah's door. "*Hodi?*" he shouted.

There was a moment's pause. Then he heard Elijah's voice. *"Hodi."*

Royce shoved the door open and stepped inside. Elijah was sitting on his bed, warming his hands over a small charcoal stove. He still wore the inevitable tinted glasses.

Royce stood there dripping. "Elijah, I know you're tired. I'm tired too. But there's a lot of work to be done."

Elijah sighed. "We cannot stop the rain, Mr. Royce."

Royce felt a brief irritation. He stifled it. "You have all done very well. I appreciate it. But we have to protect the pumps and the generator. The baboon cages have to be moved. We can't just sit in our houses and wait for better days."

Elijah said nothing.

"I want the men out, Elijah. I want you on the cages—we'll have to move them into the shed. I want Mutisya to take charge of getting some runoff ditches built around the pumps and the generator. Have Mr. Donaldson's men gone back to their camp?"

"They are not here, Mr. Royce."

"Well, they'll have their hands full with those tents. I'll check later and see if they need any food. Let's get with it, Elijah."

Elijah moved slowly, but he moved. He shrugged into a plastic raincoat that had been supplied by the Baboonery and stepped out into the rain with obvious reluctance. Royce followed him out.

It was a bad day.

The men were tired and they worked in a kind of stupor. Royce had to ride herd on all of them, directing each job in time-consuming detail. Only Mutisya and Mbali showed any initiative at all.

Royce kept his temper under control. There were times when the Africans drew away from him, retreating into their own values and their own ways. It did no good to shout at them. Of course, their own jobs were at stake in keeping the Baboonery operational, but he refrained from pointing this out. They had their own problems; he could not expect them to view things through his eyes. He kept a smile on his face and did the major share of the work without complaint. They needed each other. He would be up the creek if the men turned surly. They would be in trouble if the power failed and they just sat in their rooms waiting for something to happen. Royce ducked in and told Wathome to fix an unusually hearty dinner, and he set aside a case of precious beer to give the men with their evening meal.

Somehow, he got the job done.

The baboons were moved into the shed. Baboons, like all large primates, were very susceptible to respiratory ailments. He couldn't leave them out where the rain swept through their cages. It took four men on each cage to lift them. The wet, angry animals kept trying to grab the shoulders of the carriers, which didn't help any. That was normal, though. Royce examined the baboons closely but saw nothing unusual about them. They were just baboons— unlovely, ill-tempered, nasty, but not alien in any way.

They dug drainage ditches around the pumps and the generator and used empty shipping crates to shore up the weak points. It was hard, back-breaking work. They were

all soaked to the skin before nightfall. It made little difference whether a man kept his raincoat on or took it off. If
he kept it on, his sweat drenched him from inside. If he
took it off, the rain pelted him unmercifully. Royce took
his off by early afternoon. The rain at least was cool.

All that day, he forced himself to keep alert. He did
not know exactly what he was watching for, but he was
confident that he could recognize anything unusual if he
saw it. He spotted nothing suspicious.

When it was too dark to work further, he stumbled
into the main building. He was very tired; the last two
days had taken their toll. He didn't really want any dinner
but he made himself change into dry clothes and eat
something.

"Daddy," Susan said happily, "the roof is leaking."

"Daddy will fix it tomorrow," he said.

He fell into bed before the after-dinner coffee came.
He knew that he was courting disaster by going to sleep
before he had established any sort of a guard, but he had to
take a chance. He could not stay awake himself. The men
were as tired as he was. It was raining so hard that visibility
was close to zero.

He slept instantly.

Once, deep in the night, a sudden stillness awakened
him. For a moment, he couldn't figure out what it was.
Then he realized that the rain had stopped. Moonlight
was streaming in through the curtains. He could hear a
distant roaring over the light drip of the water from the
sodden thatch on the roof. Sleep-fogged, his tired brain
puzzled over the strange sound. It came to him that the

roaring must be the Kikumbuliu River. Only a few hours ago, or so it seemed, the Kikumbuliu had been a narrow trickle of water that he could drive a Land Rover through. It must be a raging torrent now.

He stared at the moonlight. Maybe the rain had stopped for good. Maybe, in the morning, the sun would shine.

He knew that he should get up and take a look around. He started to sit up in the bed. Kathy pushed him down again. "I'm awake," she said. "I'll call you if there's any need. Go back to sleep."

Exhausted, he slept again.

He dreamed no dreams.

Royce slept until nearly ten o'clock the next morning and when he woke up it took an effort for him to get out of bed. It was raining again; he could hear it thudding on the roof thatch. It didn't seem to be coming down quite as hard as the day before, but it was raining steadily. The whole room had a damp smell to it.

He listened for the thumping of the generator and was faintly reassured when he heard it. At least they still had power.

He went in to eat his breakfast.

"Welcome to Noah's Ark," Kathy said.

"We've got the baboons," he said. "That's a start."

He ate his breakfast slowly. Each item of food had now become a thing to be appreciated and savored. Coffee, cream, eggs, bacon, bread—when they were gone, that was it. A man could hunt in that swamp out there for a long, long time without finding a chicken or a pig, to say nothing of coffee or wheat. He might find a cow if he were lucky, but it wasn't likely. The Kamba would keep their herds close to home; there was no need to search for water now.

It was curious, Royce thought. The Baboonery had always seemed a lonely kind of place to him, stuck out in the middle of the African bush. By most standards, it had been isolated from the first. But it was different now, very different. There was no lifeline to connect him with the outside world. He could not pile in the Land Rover and go to Mitaboni for tobacco or milk. He could not depend on the train to bring in needed supplies. He couldn't even get a letter out.

He was beginning to understand the meaning of true isolation. He didn't like it, but it did not panic him. He told himself that a century ago things had not been so very different for some of his own ancestors in Texas. There had been small settlements and farms and ranches in his own state as remote as the Baboonery was now. There had been fires and floods and sickness and Comanches. Whatever it was that had come down out of the sky to threaten him, it was not more mysterious or more deadly than the Indians had seemed to his own people less than one hundred years ago. It was a strange thought, and an oddly comforting one.

If his ancestors had endured, he could do the same. Surely, he had not become that much less of a man in a mere hundred years.

"Did you catch the news?"

"I caught it. You can see most of it outside. It's raining all over Kenya. The roads are all knocked out and a lot of the bridges are already gone. It's a real dilly."

"How's the roof holding out?"

"Not bad, considering. We've got about a dozen leaks."

"I'll see what I can do. I have a sneaking sort of suspicion that we won't be going anywhere for a spell."

"Just try to take it a little easy today. I'd feel a hell of a lot safer if I didn't have a dead man in bed with me at night."

"There's some life in the old boy yet."

"See that it stays there. You know how we modern women are. Restless, unsatisfied, pampered—I may take up with a baboon."

"You won't find them very effective."

"Maybe not. But I can write my memoirs and make a fortune."

"Not a chance. *Beauty and the Baboon*—it'd be so tame these days that nobody would pay any attention to it."

"We could make it a female baboon, a crazy mixed-up baboon girl with a grudge against the world, a baboon raised from infancy by a Chinese spy. . . ."

Royce grinned. "Knock it off. I'm going up on the roof and dig in the thatch."

"Very symbolic," Kathy said.

Royce went out into the rain, feeling better than he had any right to feel. Everything looked normal, aside from a certain bottom-of-the-sea impression. It was possible, he supposed, that *they* were hampered by the rain just as he was. It couldn't be easy for them to maneuver in an alien environment. They had shown that they could operate under dry conditions, but perhaps the mud and the water would slow them down. Baboons, too, did not take well to heavy rains. . . .

He checked the generator and the pumps and got Elijah to do some more work on the drainage ditches. He found Mutisya and told him to keep an eye out for game. If they were going to be cut off for any length of time, they had to have meat.

Then he went to work on the roof. He plugged the leaks as quickly as he could, not taking the time to do the job properly. There was other work to do before nightfall.

He needed more lights. The hours of darkness were long and dangerous. The baboon cages had been tampered with at night, Kilatya had been killed at night, the bush had been fired at night. He had a light on a pole next to the generator, another one over the door to the building that housed the operating room, and a third light between the kitchen and the men's barracks. The area in front of the Baboonery depended on the light that filtered through the windows of the main building, and that wasn't good enough. There was a guest house out there, a square thatched structure that was little more than a bedroom and a bathroom. It was already wired for electricity. If he could rig up a light socket above the door, keep a bulb burning there at night . . . well, it might be useful.

He had to do *something*.

He collected the necessary gear from the supply room,

which was next to his office, and walked through the pelting rain to the guest house. He hadn't been in there for a long time. It was never used except by the visiting doctors, and there hadn't been any doctors around for quite a spell. The little house was damp but oddly stuffy despite the open windows. It had a smell of loneliness and disuse about it. A great king-sized bed that stood several feet off the floor dominated the room. It was neatly made up, ready for a giant. Kathy always referred to it as the Orgy Bed, but Royce had never tried it out.

He went to work, and the job proved to be easier than he had anticipated. He had plenty of time to think.

The rain mocked him as he worked. There was nothing dramatic about it—just a steady rain drumming on the thatch over his head and splashing into the muddy earth outside. There was no thunder, no lightning, no high wind. There was just a constant reminder that he was trapped, trapped by a combination of the most ancient of the elements and something so new that his world lacked even the words to discuss it sensibly.

Of course, his whole evaluation of the situation might be faulty. He recognized that. He could not *prove* that something had come down out of the sky and landed out there in the African bush. He could not *prove* that the strange events around the Baboonery had been connected with that landing, assuming that the landing had really happened. On the other hand, he could not prove that the sun—however obscured by clouds—would rise tomorrow either, or that the lights in the night sky were stars. The best that any man had to go on was a very high degree of probability. It was folly to act on any assumption except the one that seemed to fit the facts best. *All* explanations had once been fantastic guesses. There had been a time when it had been little short of lunacy to believe that fire could be produced from friction, that an arrow could be as deadly as a spear, that animals could be domesticated more easily than hunting them wild, that plants would grow from seeds, that the world was round. People and tribes and nations had perished from wishful thinking. The ones that survived had learned to look facts in the eye and draw the unpopular conclusions.

If something had landed here, it had not been an accident. Surely, beings that could pilot a ship across the light-years of interstellar space could select a landing place with precision. Even in the unlikely event that only inter-planetary distances had been involved, the same point would apply. Even man, with his primitive space technology, could land on a designated spot on the moon with some accuracy.

Question: Why land *here?*

Well, Royce thought, turn the thing around. Suppose that man had the capacity to explore an inhabited planet. Suppose that he was uncertain what kind of a reception he might receive. Would he plop himself down smack in the middle of a city? Or would he try to check things out first in a relatively empty area?

Of course, the chosen area should not be *completely* deserted. If you want to find out something about the natives you have to have a few to watch.

In a way, the Baboonery was ideal. It was particularly

ideal if *they* were unsure of themselves, uncertain how well they could function on this alien world. There must be limits to what you can discover from a spaceship. Sooner or later, you must test your theories. You must open your door and check things out. You have to start somewhere.

All well and good. *Except* that he could not know their motives, any more than Montezuma could understand what Cortes was after or a chimpanzee could understand why he had been rocketed into space. *Except* that it did not explain the odd incidents with the baboons or the death of Kilatya or the fire.

When you don't know what is coming, you have to be ready for anything.

Royce screwed the bulb—only 100 watts, but it was the biggest he had—into the socket he had rigged and tried it out. Somewhat to his surprise, it worked perfectly.

It wasn't much—little more than a gesture, perhaps.

But he would be able to see a little farther into the darkness, and that was something.

Royce was finishing a late lunch when Mutisya called out to him.

"Mr. Royce! *Choroa!*"

"Oryx," Royce said, getting to his feet. "Meat, if we're lucky. Make sure Elijah switches on the lights if I'm not back by dark."

"You *be* back," Kathy said.

Royce grabbed his raincoat and the .375 and ran outside. The rain was still coming down but the visibility was good enough so that he could see to shoot if he could just get a target.

"*Wapi?*" he asked. "Where?"

Mutisya pointed down the road toward Matt Donaldson's camp. "Just now I saw him. A good one. Alone."

Royce hesitated only a moment. There wasn't anything much left of the road; the Land Rover could not make it through mud that thick. Too noisy anyhow, probably. He looked at Mutisya. The Kamba stood quietly, a dignified figure somehow despite the gnarled bare feet and baggy shorts and the battered olive-colored army-surplus overcoat he wore instead of a raincoat. "Can we get him, Mutisya?"

Mutisya smiled, showing his filed pointed teeth. "I will find him. You will shoot him."

"Okay, let's go."

Mutisya started off at an easy jog, his bare feet almost silent in the mud. Royce pulled his hat down more firmly on his head and followed him. The mud sucked at his boots and he sounded like an elephant. He veered off to the side of the road where the ground was higher and firmer and tried to pace himself. Mutisya was tireless, despite his age. The man's legs were as thin as sticks, but the long muscles in them were as tough as ropes.

It was eerie once they got into the bush—a dark, dripping world of long silences and glistening wet-black bark. The sky was close and gray, pressing down upon them. The rain-streaked air was heavy and still and Royce was sweating before he had covered one hundred yards. There was an expectant hush that hovered over the sodden earth like an electrical charge. Royce could almost see the vegetation coming to life—the bushes and the grass and the trees and the creepers, all of them drinking in the rain, waiting for the magic touch of the sun to explode into leaf and flower.

Tracking was simple enough as long as the oryx stayed in the road. The marks of his hooves in the mud were so clear that a child could have followed him.

Mutisya stopped suddenly and pointed to his left.

Royce nodded, panting. The oryx had turned off here, veering into the dripping bush to avoid Donaldson's camp. He could still make out the tracks but they were fainter now; the tangle of ground-hugging plants kept the animal's feet out of the mud. The spacing of the tracks showed that the oryx had increased his speed a little, but he was not running yet.

Mutisya left the road, moving fast, his body bent over almost double. He looked for all the world as though he were sniffing out the trail. Royce kept behind him, picking open spaces, keeping his head up. Mutisya could track better than he could; Royce's job was to look ahead to see if he could spot the animal.

Mutisya saw him first, though. Some sixth sense made him look up and he stopped at once, pointing.

Royce followed the pointing finger, saying nothing. It took him a moment and then the oryx seemed to leap into view. The animal was standing quietly by a baobab tree, his head raised, looking back. It was a long shot in the rain, better than two hundred yards.

Royce lifted the heavy rifle to his shoulder and

slipped off the safety. He glued his eye to the scope. It took him a long agonizing minute to find the animal again in the scope, but then he had him. The two long, almost straight horns gave the oryx the look of a unicorn unless he was looking straight at you. He was a big animal, four hundred pounds or so, and there was power in that stout brownish-gray body. There were black and white markings on his face, and his black tufted tail was twitching slightly.

Royce took a bead just above the left shoulder and his finger tightened on the trigger.

The oryx moved. His didn't move fast or far, but he moved enough. He was screened by foliage. Royce knew about where he was, but he had no shot.

"Damn," he whispered. He lowered the rifle, wishing that he had a stand to steady his arm. The .375 was a heavy gun and a slight waver could make a big difference at that range. He had waited an instant too long. Next time . . .

He started ahead and to his right, trying to get an angle from which he could catch a glimpse of the oryx. He moved quietly, with Mutisya behind him now, taking advantage of every bit of cover he could find. He kept holding his breath and had to remind himself to breathe. He wanted that oryx. There was a lot of meat on him, enough meat to make a difference.

He thought he had lost him and then, quite suddenly, he spotted him again. The oryx was moving away and to his left. It wasn't a clear shot, but the animal was picking up speed. It was as good a shot as he was going to get.

Royce jerked the rifle up, peered through the scope,

and squeezed the trigger. The loud crack of the big rifle seemed muffled in the rain but there was nothing subdued about the kick of the gun against his shoulder.

He lowered the rifle; he could not tell what was happening through the scope. The oryx, he thought, had jerked a little with the impact of the slug—but he couldn't be sure. In any event, the animal had not gone down. The oryx turned and broke into a run, headed straight for the Kikumbuliu. Royce snapped off another shot, hoping for a miracle. There was no miracle. The oryx kept going and was lost to sight in an instant.

They ran toward the spot where the oryx had been, not worrying about the noise now. It was hard going and Royce tore his raincoat in three places. He pulled up, finally, his chest heaving.

Mutisya found the torn-up patch in the mud first, and then the bright red smear of blood; the blood was fairly thick. They found another spot a short distance away. The rain splashed into the blood and trickled off as though it had fallen into a puddle of oil.

This was where the hunting got tough.

Mutisya took the lead again. He went slowly at first, watching for the smears of blood, but then he broke into a jog. The wounded animal was running in a straight line, headed for the river. He couldn't cross it, of course, but if he just didn't turn aside until he became weak and confused . . .

Royce ran in a kind of trance, one hand clutching his rifle and the other holding his raincoat tightly against his body so that it would not catch in the bush. The rain-pounded world was dreamlike in its emptiness; nothing seemed to move, and the only sound Royce heard was the rising roar of the river.

He saw the Kikumbuliu: a swollen brown giant of a river, choked with mud and brush and uprooted trees, a river that hissed and boomed and ripped at its banks. They started down the slope. The footing was tricky; the grade that led to the river had only a dead grass cover and the ground had turned into a slippery swamp.

Mutisya stopped and threw up his hand.

Royce snapped back to alertness. The oryx was in plain sight and less than a hundred yards away. He just stood there in the pelting rain, his back to the torrent of the river, his front legs wide apart for balance. His head was up, nodding slightly, as though the weight of his horns had become a burden too heavy to bear. He was looking at Royce, waiting.

Royce steadied himself, lifted the rifle, and fired once. The oryx crumped in a heap.

The two men picked their way across the muddy earth and looked down at the animal. He was dead, his soft brown eyes already glazing. Royce's first shot had hit him in the belly. His last shot had gone home in the chest.

"Well," Royce said. "Now the fun starts."

Mutisya grinned. "He is a big one. Very heavy."

Royce took off his hat and wiped the sweat from his eyes. The two of them could not possibly pack that animal back to the Baboonery. They would have to hack him up where he lay, and even then they would need more men.

They were not far from the Baboonery—less than a mile, if one happened to be a bird.

He glanced up at the sky, letting the rain splash against his face. The clouds were black and heavy and it was beginning to get darker. There wasn't much time.

"Mutisya, I'll stay here and start cutting him up. Leave me that knife of yours and you get back to the Baboonery as fast as you can. If everything is okay there, come right back with four men and some pangas. Understand?"

"Okay, Mr. Royce."

Mutisya turned without a world of complaint and moved with his effortless stride back up the slope. He had vanished in less than a minute.

Royce fished out his pipe and got it going. He stood quietly for a moment. The rain continued to fall, cloaking the earth in sheets of silver. He was awed at the primordial loneliness that surrounded him. He thought: *I'll remember this time and this place. One day, if I'm lucky, it will all come back to me, fresh and new with the smell of rain. One day, when I need it, I'll take out this picture and see it again.*

He stared at the surging power of the dirty water in the Kikumbuliu. The once tiny stream was a great wide river, and the yellow-brown current was deep and strong. It carried broken black trees along like matchsticks, and its voice was a swirling snarl of fury. Nothing was going to cross that river for a long time to come. He could imagine what the Tsavo must look like now, and the Athi that separated him from Nairobi. And there were other rivers, too many rivers, too many little creeks and formerly dry canyons that were bursting with water. . . .

He picked up Mutisya's knife and knelt by the oryx. This was a part of hunting that saddened him. There was death where there had been life, and the thrill was gone.

He went to work.

By the time that Mutisya returned with the men— who laughed and shouted when they saw the oryx—it was almost too dark to see. They hacked the animal crudely into sections with their pangas; they could carve it up properly when they got back to the Baboonery. Within twenty minutes, they had most of the edible meat piled into canvas carrying slings.

They started back through the darkness.

Royce could see the halo of the Baboonery lights ahead of him. He felt an icy chill that had nothing to do with the cooling of the night when he became aware of the presence of the *other* light as well. It was coming from the same place that he had first seen it, a seeming eternity ago. A soft, steady, pale glow, almost like moonlight.

They were still there.

Royce was very tired. He tried to concentrate on walking, on just putting one foot after the other in the mud. His brain was numbed. He was beyond mere worry.

He stared at those two lights shining through the darkness and the rain: two lights that were utterly different, separated by more than distance, and yet somehow linked.

We're all in this together, he thought.

Wearily, he put his head down.

He was going home. He held that thought in his head. He was going home, a hunter carrying his meat. He was at the end of an inconceivably long procession of men, stretching back through the ages, men returning from hunts long forgotten. . . .

It was, somehow, a comforting thought.

There was a tie with the past, a continuity, no matter what the future might hold.

8

THE LONG DAYS passed, and the longer nights. The rain kept coming. It did not rain continuously—the sun even broke through the clouds a few times—but it rained enough so that the earth had no chance to dry out. The rivers roared and water dripped in a steady stream from the roof thatch. Clothing mildewed in the dresser drawers. The moist planks of the walls were streaked with mold. Outside, the world was a dismal gray, as though the rain had absorbed all colors and all life. The skies were gray, the bush was gray, even the mud was gray. The mud had been red once, the color of rust, but the red was gone along with the clouds of dust that had once hung in the sun-baked air.

Royce waited. There was very little else that he could do. Supplies were running a little low, but they were in no danger from that quarter yet. The meat from the oryx had helped. He still had plenty of fuel for the generator. The children were both healthy now, although they were cross and bored. The novelty of the rain had worn off, and Kathy had her hands full trying to entertain them.

There were nights when the strange pale glow was plainly visible, and there were other nights when the bush surrounding the Baboonery was black and still and lifeless.

Royce toyed with the idea of tracking that light down. He knew he could find the source if he put enough effort into it. He would have tried it if he had been alone; he was desperately curious about what must be out there in the bush, and he knew that there was a chance he might find out something that would be useful to him. But he could not risk it. As long as *they* did not attack him he was prepared to leave them alone. To go out there after them was asking for trouble. He could probably do nothing even if he found them, and if he got himself killed Kathy and the children would be in a hopeless position. That game wasn't worth the candle.

He waited, not knowing what to expect. Most of his fears were centered vaguely around the possibility of a direct attack under the cover of darkness. He was not quite ready for what actually happened.

It was daylight and a gentle rain was falling. Most of the men were in their quarters. Royce was standing at the kitchen window, looking out. A single baboon ran suddenly out of the bush and headed straight for the building that housed Royce's office and the operating rooms. For a long moment, Royce did not react. He noticed that the animal was wet and bedraggled and thin almost to the point of emaciation. The baboon darted into the building. By the time Royce had snatched up his rifle and lunged out the door, the baboon was outside again. The animal clutched a couple of pineapples to his chest and scurried away in a queer three-legged run. Royce snapped off one shot, missed, and the baboon disappeared back into the bush.

On the surface, that was all there was to it.

Royce, however, learned some important things from the seemingly trivial pineapple raid. It was highly unlikely that a normal baboon would behave as that animal had done. Baboons often helped themselves to a farmer's maize crop standing in the field, but they seldom ran through an occupied area and into a building after food. That was highly unusual, to say the least. If Royce had needed any additional evidence that some alien intelligence was controlling the baboons, he now had it.

More crucially, the incident taught him something that he should have realized before. If *they* had somehow taken over the baboons—not all of the baboons, of course, but some of them—the reason for the takeover was obvious. They could not function on this world without elaborate protective devices any more than a man could go for a stroll on Jupiter in his birthday suit. They had to work through a native animal, one that was already adapted to the environment of this planet. A baboon was a primate, like a man. A little simpler, a little easier . . .

They were practicing. The baboons were a means, not an end. A way station, a halfway house. . . .

But if you take over a baboon and control him, that animal must still *live* as a baboon. He must eat, find shelter, ward off disease, protect himself from his enemies.

Normally, he can do this readily enough. But if you short-circuit his brain, if you interpose an alien intelligence, what then? It is no help to a baboon to know philosophy or interstellar navigation. He has to know what insects to eat, which plants are nourishing, where the rock shelters are, how to avoid leopards.

The rains make things complicated, for baboons as well as men.

The baboon that had gone after the stored pineapples must have been desperate for food. He did not know even *what* to eat, much less where to find it. All he knew was that the captive baboons were fed maize and pineapple, and that traps were set with the same foods. The only certain source of those foods within miles was the Baboonery storeroom.

The next step was so glaringly obvious that Royce distrusted it on principle. Still, he could not afford to ignore it. He knew that a really hungry animal was a stupid animal. Even a deer will take long chances when his belly has been empty long enough.

Royce gave instructions that the outside door of the building that contained the storeroom was to be left slightly ajar. He locked the storeroom itself. He filled the syringe that was fastened to the pole with sernyl and put it in the lab, which was in the same building with the storeroom. From the inside, he unfastened the bottom of the lab window screen. The window was on the opposite side of the building from the bush where the baboons were.

He left the building by the door, went into the main building, and made himself a couple of sandwiches. Carrying the sandwiches and his rifle, he went outside again, this time using the front door. It was raining harder, and his boots squished into the mud. He walked a short distance through the muck that had once been the main road, left the road, and doubled back. He climbed through the window of the lab, refastened the screen, and sat down to wait. He kept his rifle ready on a lab table beside him, but he had the syringe pole in his hand. He didn't want another dead baboon. He wanted one of those creatures alive.

He sat there for hours, listening to the rain drumming on the roof. Absolutely nothing happened. He waited until almost dark and gave up. He could not risk it alone in the lab at night unless he turned the lights on. He left the building, locked the outside door, and posted a guard.

The next morning, he tried his trick again.

Royce crouched behind the lab door, annoyed with himself because his hands were trembling. He heard Mutisya's shout and then a rapid scurrying sound in the hallway. He could not be certain, but from the amount of noise he judged that there was more than one animal in the corridor. He forced himself to wait, his heart thudding in his chest.

He heard a scratching sound as the animals tried the locked storeroom door. He knew that the creatures would have to move fast; if they could not open the storeroom door they would have to retreat quickly to have any hope of escaping. He waited until he heard them pass the lab door again.

Now.

He jerked open the door and sprinted into the hallway. There was a stench of baboons in the corridor. He saw
them—two wet and skinny animals running for the open
outside door. Royce did not hesitate. Just as the lead
baboon ran through the door, Royce caught up with the
other one. He jabbed the syringe into his rear end and
jammed the plunger home. The baboon turned with a
coughing snarl. Royce yanked out the bent needle and
thrust the sturdy pole into the animal's chest, hurling him
back. The baboon snapped at the pole with his long white
teeth.

Royce dropped the pole, turned, and ran back into the
lab. He slammed the door and locked it and snatched up
his rifle. There was a thud as the animal's body struck the
lab door. Royce did not fire. He stood there, rifle ready,
catching his breath. He heard the baboon racing up and
down the corridor. The animal was confused now, afraid
to venture outside and trapped if he stayed in.

The sernyl began to take effect. Gradually, the baboon's movements slowed, became erratic. There was a
long pause. Royce heard a sodden thump as the animal fell
to the floor.

Royce waited a long minute, then opened the lab
door. There was a smell of excrement in the hallway. The
baboon was out cold, a huddled gray heap on the mud-
spattered floor. He was breathing rapidly, the fangs bared
in his long snout.

Royce felt a moment of pity for the creature. Whatever
it had become, it had reached the end of a long and

strange journey. In its own mind, it must have believed itself cornered by alien beings in an alien land. It had been wet and hungry and afraid.

"Well, pal," Royce said softly, "I didn't ask you to come here. Remember that."

He went outside into a driving rain. The other baboon had escaped back to the bush. Royce told Elijah to have the men carry a strong cage into the lab. When they got it into position, Royce and Mutisya lifted the unconscious animal into the cage. Royce put food and water in the cage, fastened the door, and put a padlock on it.

He instructed Mutisya to keep a sharp lookout and told Elijah that he would hold him responsible if anyone harmed the baboon. Then he locked the lab and locked the building and went inside to eat lunch.

There was nothing to do now except wait for the creature to recover.

As he ate his lunch, listening with half an ear to the chatter of his children, he was far from certain as to what his course of action should be.

He had his baboon, true enough. There remained the small problem of what the devil he was going to do with him.

Royce returned to the lab and hitched a chair up close to the cage—but not too close. He took out his pipe, filled it with Sweet Nut, and got it going. The rain pattered on the roof with a steady monotonous beat. A large black spider, like a burned pancake with legs, walked calmly across the floor and disappeared under a cabinet.

The baboon was awake. He sat in the far corner of the cage, as far as he could get from Royce, and stared at the man. The animal had eaten some of its food. He was an unlovely beast at best, and he smelled. Of all the primates, Royce thought, the baboon was the least attractive. A man felt an instant kinship with a chimpanzee, and gorillas could be charming despite their formidable size. Gibbons were endearing creatures, and orangs were fun in a lugubrious sort of way. Most of the monkeys were pleasant enough, if a trifle blunt in their manners. Lemurs looked like pets with their bushy tails, and tarsiers were clowns with their hopping legs and great saucer eyes. But it was hard to feel affection for a baboon. They were ugly and they could be dangerous, but it was more than that. The baboon lived on the ground, like man. The two animals had been competitors, perhaps for a million years and more. . . .

The animal in the cage was not a baboon, not any longer. Royce knew that, and the cold intelligence that looked out through the creature's eyes was all the proof that he needed. But he *looked* like a baboon. It took an effort of will to think of him as anything else.

Royce puffed on his pipe and felt singularly futile. He was almost close enough to reach out and touch the creature but there was no basis for contact. He did not even know whether or not *they* had a language, much less what it was. There was no convenient telepathy. He could not bring himself to utter, even in jest, the classic stock line: "Do you speak English?" Or Swahili, perhaps. Or Urdu. The idea was absurd.

He went to the storeroom, got a pineapple, and approached the cage. The animal snarled, watching him closely. Royce extended his hand, offering the pineapple. The creature defecated in fear. Royce put the pineapple in the cage and went back to his chair. The thing that looked like a baboon stared at him with something like horror and did not move.

Royce studied him as well as he could. The animal did not look healthy. His coat was dull, his eyes cloudy. He was too thin and there were vermin around his ears. Baboons were social animals; they lived in bands. A baboon alone, cut off from his society, would have a difficult time of it.

"You poor bastard," Royce said. "I'm not enjoying this."

He did not know whether or not he could keep the creature alive. Now that he had him, he was not sure that it was a good idea to keep him around at all. Would the others come after him? And *how* would they come—as baboons or as something else?

It seemed to Royce, as he sat there looking at the thing in the cage, that he had been wrong in thinking that *they* were simply controlling the baboons in some way. Surely, if that were the case, they could withdraw their control from an injured or captured animal. For that matter, they could release the baboons to forage naturally, then reimpose their control when it was needed.

It didn't work that way.

He knew that they had to catch a baboon and take it to their ship in order to use it. It took some time. And that meant . . .

They were not just manipulating the baboons. They

were *in* the baboons. There must be some sort of transplant involved, perhaps an actual replacement of the brain. . . .

He looked at the creature in the cage. He stared at the sick, alien eyes. He felt a sudden, irrational chill of dread. He was in the same room with one of *them*, face to face with . . . what?

"My God," he whispered. "Who are you? Why have you come here? What do you want?"

Royce thought: *He knows things I cannot know. He does not think as I think. He is trapped in a crazy body, locked in a cage, but he is smarter than I am. He might be able to do . . . anything.*

Slowly, almost mindlessly, his hand reached out for the rifle. Then he hesitated, stopped. He cared nothing for the scientific value of the creature now; his problem was survival. But shooting a baboon was one thing, and murdering an alien intelligence was something else.

He sat there, frozen into inaction, one hand touching the rifle.

A voice from outside: "Mr. Royce! Mr. Royce!"

He got to his feet, taking his rifle with him. He left the lab, locking the door behind him. He hurried through the corridor and out the door. He locked that door too.

The men were gathered in a knot by the baboon cages under the shed. Several of them were armed with bows and arrows. Royce ran through the rain and joined them.

"What is it, Mutisya?"

The African pointed at the bush. "Out there. Many baboons. Listen—you can hear them."

Royce held his breath. The patter of the rain and the muted roar of the distant river covered up all other sounds. He knew that his hearing was not as sharp as Mutisya's. He tried, straining hs ears. He thought he heard a coughing and barking in the bush but he could not be sure.

He could see, though. He peered through the silver-gray sheets of rain at the dark and dripping bush. He saw shadows there, moving shadows.

"Our friend has company," he said. He stroked the barrel of his rifle, wiping off the raindrops with his fingers. Those shadows were within range. But if he shot them, what then? He had not forgotten the strange sharp tracks that he had seen. *They* could move with their natural forms encased in armor, he figured—unless the mud prevented them. For that matter, they could probably lift their ship unless they had had an accident of some kind. They could wipe him out from the air as easily as he could swat a fly. . . .

One baboon-thing emerged from the bush. He advanced slowly across the clearing, moving gingerly, reluctantly. He stopped, started to go back to the safety of the bush, then came on again. Royce watched him with a grudging admiration. Either the animal was mad or . . .

Before Royce could act, a Kamba fitted an arrow to his bow and loosed the shaft. The feathered arrow whistled through the wet air. Considering the range, it was a fairly near miss. The poisoned shaft arced down within fifteen yards of the animal.

The baboon turned and ran for cover. The men laughed and slapped one another on the back.

Royce felt a quick surge of relief. He was not sure how to proceed, but he was suddenly certain that they were on the wrong track. A full-scale battle could have only one ultimate outcome, even if they managed to kill *all* of the baboon-things. There had to be a better way.

"That was a good shot," he said. "But I don't want to fight them unless they give us no other choice. Mutisya, I want you to stand guard here with your best bowmen. Don't let them move in close. Elijah, I want four men to help me carry the cage out of the lab."

Elijah looked at him his eyes hidden behind his rain-spotted glasses. "What is your plan?"

"I want to let him go."

Elijah shook his head. "Mr. Royce, that is wrong. Never fight a war with your finger. If you catch a Masai and release him he will not thank you. He will be back with his spear."

Royce hesitated. He had no right to give orders to these men when their own lives might be at stake. It was true that they could not understand the situation, but he could not be sure of his own tactics either.

"Those baboons are sick," he said. "They are not like other baboons. I think the sickness came down out of the sky. You know that we are trapped here by the rain—you are cut off from your people and I am cut off from mine. I am not trying to play the *bwana mkubwa* just because you happen to work for me. One of us must make the decisions. If you trust me, I will make them. If you do not, you can do what you think best. I am afraid that if we keep that sick baboon in the cage the others will fight to take him away. If we let him go, they may let us alone. I may be wrong, but if we let him go and they keep on coming anyway we are no worse off than we are now. Does that make sense to you, Elijah?"

The headman did not answer him directly. He walked off to one side and conferred with the other men. They talked a long time. Then Elijah came back with four men. He smiled. "Okay, Mr. Royce."

Royce said nothing more. He led them into the lab and they picked up the cage by the carrying rods. It was heavy and the creature in the cage snarled at them. Royce could smell his diseased odor. He could feel the stiffening of his hair on his scalp, feel an unreasoning terror. The thing was so close. . . .

They walked slowly across the clearing with the other men fanning out on either side. Royce peered ahead into the bush but saw nothing. They set the cage down at the far edge of the clearing.

"Go on back and cover me," Royce said. "I'll let him out."

The men retreated to the shelter of the shed without argument.

Royce checked his rifle and slipped the safety off. He unlocked the padlock and unfastened the cage door. He prodded the door open a little with the rifle barrel and stood back.

The creature in the cage stared at him with sick, puzzled eyes. It made no move.

"Come on," Royce said. "I'm not going to hurt you."

The baboon-thing bared his fangs at the sound of his voice but still made no move.

Royce began to back away, his rifle ready. He backed a

good forty yards across the clearing, his eyes fixed on the cage. Then he turned and ran through the mud to the shed. Standing with the other men, he saw the rain-blurred shadow of the baboon as it left the cage and disappeared into the bush.

"Go tell your friends," Royce muttered.

He locked up the storeroom building and wearily plodded through the muck toward the breezeway. He was wet and discouraged. There seemed to be no significant action that he could take. He had perhaps postponed a showdown but that was not good enough.

He could not wait indefinitely.

He had to *do* something.

When he had cleaned himself up and changed clothes, he went to locate Kathy. He found her in the kitchen supervising Wathome's cooking. Wathome preferred to do his cooking alone, but he had discovered that Kathy was less tractable than his own three wives. Royce sympathized with him, and he had a sneaking suspicion that Wathome pitied him for his inability to keep his woman in line.

Royce eased Kathy into the sitting room. He suggested to Barbara and Susan, who had their junk spread all over the dining room table, that they go and play in the bedroom. His suggestion met with a very cool reception, and he decided to let them stay where they were. The children were bored and fretful and the issue wasn't worth a fuss.

Outside, the rain had slowed to a gentle drizzle.

"I've got an idea," he said.

Kathy had dark shadows under her eyes. She looked older. Her hand trembled slightly as she lit one of her last cigarettes. "I think I'm about ready for it, whatever it is."

"I think there may be a way to get out of here."

"Don't build it up. Just tell me."

He took a deep breath. "Look, we've forgotten about something. We can't make Nairobi or Machakos. We can't make Hunter's or Mac's because of the rivers. We can't even make Mitaboni. *But we don't have to.*"

"We can stay here, if that's what you mean. This isn't a good time for jokes, Royce. Really, your sense of timing. . ."

"We forgot about Bob Russell," Royce said quietly.

Kathy sat down on the hard leather couch. A flicker of hope showed in her eyes.

"Bob Russell's place is between here and Mitaboni. If I can get out to the main road, I'd only have nine miles to go—and that on tarmac of a sort. There's only one large draw on that stretch; I can probably get through the water. Russell has got a telephone. I could call the police in Nairobi and have them send a copter to pick us up."

Kathy drew on her cigarette. "You make it sound so simple. I'm a big girl now, Royce. You'd have to walk the whole way—that's nearly twenty miles. Russell probably got out long ago, and he probably thinks that we did, too. He wouldn't have known, or wouldn't remember, that Susan was too sick to travel. It would be a miracle if that phone was still operating. It would take you days, even if you made it. I don't want to be left alone here; I can't stand that."

Royce searched for some words and didn't find them. He did the best he could. "You won't be alone. I trust Mutisya and the others—*have* to trust them. I think I can get the Land Rover through part of the way—not all the way to the main road, but maybe a few miles. I could make it to Russell's and back in thirty-six hours easily, even if I rested up when I got there. I'd only be gone one night. It's a chance, Kathy. *And we can't just sit here.* I'm afraid to risk it any longer."

"What about me? If I could go with you . . ."

"We can't leave the kids here alone. We can't take them with us; they'd never make it. My God, Kathy, do you think I *want* to leave you sitting here? I just don't know what else to do."

"You could send Mutisya, couldn't you?"

"I considered it. He's a good man. He could get through as well as I could, maybe better. But what if Russell isn't there? Mutisya can't use a telephone. Even if he could, would he get any action? I can go all the way up to the American representatives if I have to. I'm the one who has to go, if anyone does."

Kathy ground out her cigarette. She looked at him for a long time. "Tomorrow?"

"In the morning. Early."

"I'll pack some sandwiches for you," she said.

The rain began to fall harder and a cool wind blew through the windows from out of the darkening sky.

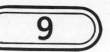

9

ROYCE LEFT WITH the first light of dawn, partly to give himself as much daylight as possible and partly with the hope that his departure would not be noticed. He had told Elijah and Mutisya of his plan the night before; he said nothing to them now. He did not awaken the children. He kissed Kathy lightly, almost casually. There were no words that he could say to her that would not sound hollow and forced.

The rain had slacked off during the late night hours. There was a fine mist in the cold morning air, but the road had drained fairly well. He had no idea how far he could get in the Land Rover, but even a few miles would help. It would save him time and it would save him strength; he would be needing both.

The Land Rover started sluggishly but the engine caught. He let it warm up for a minute or two; he didn't want to kill the engine in a crucial spot. He eyed the mud ahead of him without optimism. He took a deep breath and started out.

He kept it in two-wheel drive at first; he had no confidence in the mud gear. The vehicle fish-tailed through the muck and almost went into a spin. He hit a puddle that was virtually a miniature lake and began to lose traction. Despite his misgivings, he shoved in the mud gear. He had no choice. The low-ratio four-wheel drive would give him too much power and dig him in; the mud gear gave him less power but engaged all four wheels. The Land Rover kept going somehow and cleared the puddle.

Royce kept to the right, out of the ruts. His right wheels spun on wet grass and brush, but there was more traction there than in the slick, deep mud. He did not try to think. He just pushed the vehicle along, maintaining speed, trying not to stop. He could not maneuver; every turn of the wheel started a skid that was difficult to control. He hit rocks and roots and erosion cuts; he kept on going.

He passed the loading shed, bleak and deserted in the gray morning air, and jounced across the wet gleaming rails of the tracks. He negotiated the long sweeping curve, employing every ounce of driving skill that he had. The muddy trail was reasonably straight now. He picked up a little speed, praying that his momentum would carry him through the sticky spots.

The relatively open country was behind him; the bush closed in. He was forced almost into the ruts; there was no clearance on the side of the road. Wet branches slapped at his face. It seemed to grow darker. The great dripping baobab trees pressed in on both sides. The acacias were black as wet iron, the creepers were black and glistening snakes. He could hear the steady drip of the water above the whine of his engine.

He lost track of time. His knuckles were white on the wheel, sweat trickled from his armpits in icy streams. He hit a stump, spun off, skidded in a complete circle, kept going.

Every foot, every yard, every mile. . . .

He saw it coming, but there was nothing that he could do.

The texture of the soils beneath him changed, with sands giving way to clays. He approached a long stretch that was gray-black in color and oozing water. The trail was very narrow; there was no way he could turn off.

He increased his speed as much as he dared and hit the muck with a splashing jolt. He didn't have a chance, and knew it. The Land Rover slithered wildly and slowly as the wheels sank in. He shifted to low gear and tried to bull his way through. All forward motion stopped and the wheels spun in the slime. He could smell the scorched rubber and see the steam rising from the mud.

He put the vehicle in neutral and wiped the sweat from his face. His hands were shaking.

Think, dammit.

He might get a few yards more by putting branches under the wheel, but he could never get clear to the firmer ground that was a good hundred yards ahead of him. For that, he would need a winch, a crew of men, and about six hours of work. It was time to hoof it. But he might need the Land Rover again on the way back; he had made five or six miles since leaving the Baboonery, and that was a far piece to walk. He didn't want to leave the vehicle stuck in the mud.

He climbed out into the drizzle and went to work. His boots made sucking sounds in the deep mud. He gathered dead saturated branches and inserted them behind the wheels. He lined the worst of the patch behind him with more wood and got back into the vibrating Land Rover.

He used the low-ratio four-wheel drive this time, putting it in reverse. He gave it short, sharp bursts of gas to get the Land Rover rocking. Then, before the wheels could dig in any more deeply, he floored the gas pedal and hung on. The vehicle came up like a stranded fish and lurched back over the shattered wood. He got it on more or less solid ground, found a small opening in the bush, and backed into it. The Land Rover was ready. One sharp turn of the wheel and it was headed back toward the Baboonery.

Royce switched off the ignition and pocketed the keys.

He wasted no time. He checked the wrapped sandwiches in his raincoat pocket, patted the box of heavy bullets. He stuck a short flashlight in his belt and slung a coil of light nylon rope over his shoulder. He picked up his rifle.

He started walking. It was slow going at first as he picked his way around the edges of the deep mud, but when he was able to return to the road he made better time. He stayed on the high center and the footing was slippery but firm.

The sky overhead was a thick, solid gray; there was no trace of sunlight. The bush on both sides of him was a dark wet tangle—twisted dripping trees, columns of motionless euphorbia, clumps of brush bent over by the weight of the water. Nothing moved. He saw no animals. There were no birds in the air or on the trees. It was utterly still except for the steady drip of the water and the splashing of his own feet.

It was really very simple. He lost some time detouring around thick mud and obstructions but he made better progress than he had expected. The country gradually opened up around him; the sensation of uncluttered space was refreshing after the dense bush. Even the air felt a little lighter.

He scrambled down a deeply eroded cut that was still awash with brown water, hauled himself up the other side, and felt tarmac under his boots with a sense of relief.

He had reached the Mombasa-Nairobi road.

It was only ten o'clock. He had been gone from the Baboonery slightly more than four hours.

The road would have been murder for a car—it was pocked with deep chuckholes and sheets of water in every dip—but it was not too tough for a man on foot. Royce was able to walk at almost his normal pace.

The road was completely deserted, of course. Nothing had passed this way for a long, long time. It was an eerie feeling, walking along that empty road under the leaden morning sky. It was as though Royce had somehow slipped back in time. The spasmodic bus service, the little cars

with the men in turbans and the women in saris, the
trucks loaded with produce, the government Land Rovers,
the Africans pushing their herds of bone-thin cattle
through the red dust that fringed the road—all of it had
vanished. And before that: the missionary-explorers, walking this same route into the interior from the coast, sending out crazy reports of a snow-capped mountain not far
from the Equator. And the old slaving expeditions, the
Arabs and Swahilis plying their trade from Zanzibar to
Lake Victoria. And before them Africans like the Kambas
hauling ivory to the Indian Ocean in footsore caravans.
And beyond all that an unknown land, a world never seen,
animals so thick they covered the earth as the bison had
covered the American plains, tribes and peoples whose
very names had been lost, men and women who had lived
and died long before the Kamba and the Masai had
come. . . .

All that, right here where he walked in silence.

He was not the first to pass this way, in a hurry, his
mind troubled with desperate problems. He would not be
the last.

Royce did not push himself. He walked steadily but
he conserved his strength. There was one deep draw
between him and Russell's place. It was normally dry or
nearly dry, but it would be a river of fast water now. He
could never cross it in a weakened condition. And he had
his rifle to worry about.. . . .

Take it as it comes. Take it as it comes.

There were times when the world seemed very small.
There were times when it all came down to this: one man
and a rifle and water to cross.

A century from now, it might not matter or be remembered. A century from now, even *they* might be forgotten—or man himself might have vanished from the earth.

But it mattered now. It mattered to him: what he was, and what he might become. He was just one man, but that was all that any man could claim.

He walked on, pacing himself. His shoulders began to ache. He shifted his heavy rifle from one hand to the other. The sky grew darker and fat drops of warm rain began to fall. He welcomed the rain, tepid though it was; he was hot and sticky and his clothes were damp.

Royce heard the water before he came to it. Not the roaring of a river in flood. No, it was a softer sound, a well-oiled sound, a hiss and bubble of swift water. . . .

The road simply disappeared beneath the flow of yellow-brown water. There was no way to tell how deep it was. The current was strong and fast; there were sticks and tufts of grass and uprooted bushes rushing downstream. It had been worse: Royce could see the road damage that indicated that the water level had been far higher during the peak of the rains. There were good-sized trees strewn along the banks where they had been scattered by the force of the flow.

He estimated the width of the stream as about thirty yards. It was not an impossible distance, but Royce didn't kid himself. He knew fast water. A trout stream half that wide could knock a man down, and that was in clear water where you could see where you were going.

He stepped carefully into the water, testing it. He moved out a yard or two, sliding his feet in a fisherman's shuffle. The dirty water was up to the tops of his boots and the tug was strong. As he had suspected, the angle of dropoff was steep. It would be over his head in the middle of the river.

He backed out. There was no way he could cross here without swimming. He could not swim with a rifle, and he was not sure he could make it even without the rifle.

Royce forced himself to rest. He sat down on a rock by the side of the road. He unwrapped two cheese sandwiches and wolfed them down; they wouldn't be helped by being underwater. He fished out his pipe and got it going. The tobacco hissed when the rain hit it.

He got up after a few minutes, knocked out his pipe, and stuffed it in his pocket. He left the road and moved to his right, heading upstream. He had no idea of how far he might have to go, but he knew that the stream would have to broaden out somewhere. Drainages for flood waters seldom stayed in deep cuts; even rivers that always carried water had stretches that were wide and shallow.

It was tough going. There was no trail here, and there were places where he had to force his body through the brush. He stayed as close to the water as he could; the higher water of a few days ago had partially cleared a path for him. The mud was thick and great gobs of it stuck to his boots.

He lost nearly an hour before he found a possible crossing. He saw outcroppings of black gritty rock from an ancient lava flow and the channel of the stream widened perceptibly. The current was still very fast but it was broken into rapids and pools. There was white water mixed with brown. It had to be relatively shallow, but it was plenty deep enough to drown a man.

Royce moved another hundred yards or so upstream, giving himself plenty of room to move with the water. He found a stout tree near the bank and tied one end of the nylon rope to it. He tied the other end around his waist and carried the slack line in a coil in his left hand. He hefted the rifle in his right hand.

He started across. The bottom was good and firm. The dirty water boiled up around his legs, reached his waist. The current was strong; he could not move directly toward the opposite bank. He had to go at an angle downstream. He fought to yield as little ground as possible so that he would not run out of rope.

His right arm, holding the rifle clear of the water, began to pain him. Debris floating down the river almost knocked him from his feet. He had to move slowly, testing the bottom he could not see. For long, agonizing minutes he doubted that he could make it. He had actually reached down with his left hand to untie the rope around his waist when he hit the upward slope. The water dropped to his knees and he was able to move upstream, recovering some slack. He stumbled out of the river, put down his rifle, and tied the end of the rope to a tree. It would be easier now to cross again, if he had to.

Royce rested for a few minutes, but he was becoming concerned about time. He picked up his rifle and trudged back through the mud to the road. It was still raining but he hardly noticed.

It was almost three o'clock. It had been about nine hours since he had left the Baboonery.

Royce made steady progress along the deserted highway. He reached the Russell turnoff a little after four. The little road that led to Russell's place was not paved. Royce could tell at a glance that no vehicles had passed in or out for at least the past several days. Either Russell had cleared out early or he was still there.

Royce walked through the sticky mud with the open sisal fields on both sides of him. He was bone-weary. The driveway was a long one and it was ten minutes before he came in sight of the low stone-and-wood house with its long screened porch. He saw no signs of activity.

Royce stopped. He heard no dogs barking, and that was odd. Russell would not have taken his dogs with him; he would have left them with his African staff.

Think. This is no time to be stupid.

Royce left the road and entered the sisal field on his right. The footing was soft and the tough sisal blades were strong enough to impede his progress, but the sisal plants were tall enough to give him some cover. He worked around in a curve that would bring him in behind the house.

He got close enough to see the kitchen door. He stopped again, uncertain how to proceed. It was all very well to be careful, but it was dangerous to sneak up on the house. He was inviting one of Bob Russell's bullets in his chest. He decided to call out a greeting, but the sound never came.

He spotted them, sitting in an open shed near one of the outbuildings.

Baboons. Two of them.

Royce ducked down in the sisal, his heart hammering. He slid his rifle into position.

They *might* just be baboons venturing in around an empty house. It was possible, but he didn't believe it. And if they were not just baboons . . .

The kitchen door opened.

Bob Russell came out.

The settler moved as though he were in a daze, or in the last stages of some crippling illness. His stocky body was canted at an odd angle. His long black hair, always brushed straight back, hung like a screen over his face.

Russell shuffled toward the baboons. He passed within five feet of them. They did not react, and neither did he. Russell entered the outbuilding, which was used for equipment storage. He stayed inside a few minutes and then emerged again. He walked slowly back past the baboons, entered the kitchen door, and vanished into the house.

One baboon got to its feet. It stood there in the shed, its limp tail drooping over the patches of bare skin on its rear end. The animal made a sound that was midway between a cough and a grunt. Its long snout, emerging nakedly from the thick ruff of its neck hair, parted in a cavernous yawn. Even at that distance, Royce could tell that the animal was a male by the size of its spikelike canine teeth.

Royce got down flat in the mud between the sisal plants. The implication of what he had seen stunned him. It was obvious that *they* had not confined their attentions to the Baboonery. The creatures had found Bob Russell's place. They had been successful here. They had done . . . something . . . to Russell.

Probably, Royce thought, they had gotten to Russell

before the rains came. If they had taken a direct route through the bush, Russell's place was almost as close to them as the Baboonery. Had they taken Russell to the ship? Was it possible that they had simply worked on him *here*?

Royce bit his lip. *How* they had done it didn't matter. It was done. The problem was what to do about it.

He made himself as comfortable as he could. The rain had eased to a drizzle. With the clouds choking the sky, it would be dark in less than two hours. His chances would be better then.

He had to get into that house. There was a chance that the phone was still working. There was a chance that he might be able to help Russell; he could not just abandon the man.

Meanwhile, he could rest. He was reasonably safe where he was. He did not dare push himself to the point of exhaustion. Whatever else happened, he had to be able to get back to the Baboonery.

He cradled the wet rifle in his arms.

He lay there in the cool mud beneath the vast uncaring sky and waited.

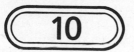

10

ROYCE CAME TO with a start. His body felt stiff and cold. The rain had stopped and there were a few early stars showing through breaks in the clouds. There was a pale light visible in Bob Russell's house. He judged that it came from the big sitting room. The kitchen was dark.

Royce did not bother with any fancy plan. If the baboon-things were watching the back of the house, they would be guarding the front as well. His best chance was to be *quick*. He checked his rifle as best he could.

He got to his feet and moved in a crouching run straight for the kitchen door. It seemed to him that his boots squishing through the mud were loud enough to be heard in Nairobi. He could not see clearly in the faint starlight, but there was no sound of alarm.

Royce grabbed the knob on the kitchen door, twisted it. The door opened. He slipped inside and closed the door quietly behind him. It took him long, slow seconds before he could see in the gloom. He crossed the kitchen and flattened himself by the side of the door that led into the house from the kitchen. On the other side of that door, he remembered, was the dining room. Beyond that was the main sitting room. Judging by the light he had seen, that was where Bob Russell was.

He stood absolutely still, trying to control his breathing. Now that he was inside, he was uncertain how to proceed. There might be some of the baboon creatures in the house. He did not know whether or not he could communicate with Russell.

He looked around him as his eyes adjusted to the darkness. There was no place in the kitchen where he could hide. There was a big iron stove and a box of wood next to it. There was a paraffin refrigerator; he could see the wick burning in the blue glass tube underneath. There was an empty wooden table with two chairs. A sink, with dishes neatly placed in a drying rack beside it. Shelves, lots of shelves. He squinted. There was the tea. There was the sugar.

Where were the Africans who worked for Russell? If they had been taken over too . . .

A sliver of yellow light showed suddenly under the dining-room door. Someone had switched on a light.

He heard Russell's voice. The words were muffled; he could not make them out. There was no reply. He heard a heavy sound as though Russell had stumbled. The light went off again.

Royce took a deep breath. He could not afford to lose any more time. He had to get close to Russell and he had to try that phone. He could accomplish nothing in the kitchen.

He crouched down, remembering the exact location of the rooms in the house.

He got his rifle into position.

Now.

He opened the dining-room door. It swung silently on its hinges. He went through, moving fast. He sensed the empty dining room around him and did not hesitate. He moved toward the light.

Royce stepped to the right through a hallway. He rounded the corner into the sitting room. He snapped the heavy rifle to his shoulder.

"Easy now, Bob," he said softly. "It's Royce. I mean you no harm. Just stay where you are."

Bob Russell was seated on the couch. There was a half-full bottle of Scotch on the long table in front of the couch. The old grandfather clock in the corner had stopped. The zebra-skin rugs on the red tile floor were dirty and twisted. The kudu head over the great fireplace was hanging crookedly.

Russell stared at him vacantly. His eyes were red beneath their bushy black brows. He needed a shave. His hard, capable hands were trembling.

Royce moved forward slowly. He lowered the rifle from his shoulder; it was too heavy and awkward to hold it that way for long. He kept it trained on Russell's torn white shirt.

"Bob! It's Royce Crawford. Can you understand me? What's happened to you?"

The settler made a strangled noise deep in his throat. He lurched to his feet, knocking the bottle off the table. There was no sign of recognition in his bloodshot eyes.

Royce took a step backward, his finger tensing on the trigger. "Hold it, Bob. I know you're not responsible . . ."

The being that looked like Bob Russell groaned. He shook his head. He advanced toward Royce, the fingers on his work-toughened hands opening and closing.

Royce felt a cold chill of horror but he could not bring himself to fire. He could not send a bullet tearing through the guts of whatever was left of a man who had been named Bob Russell. He knew that his failure to shoot was stupid but there was no time for second thoughts.

He reversed the rifle, holding it by the barrel. As Russell came closer, Royce swung the rifle butt. Russell ducked under it and the force of the swing turned Royce half around.

Before Royce could recover, Russell was on him. The hard hands dug into his shoulders, grinding against bone. Royce grunted in pain. He smelled a sick stench and there was black hair in his face. He felt a sharp burning at his throat.

My God, he thought. *He's trying to bite me!*

Royce dropped the rifle. He stopped thinking and let his reflexes take over. He twisted into position and brought his knee up, hard.

Russell shrieked an animal cry. His grip loosened. Royce pulled back a step and went for the face. He threw rights and lefts as fast as he could, more out of fear than anything else. He wanted to keep Russell away from him.

Some of the punches landed but they did no damage. Royce's arms felt like cardboard—cardboard with puffs of cotton where fists should be.

Russell shook them off. He moved in, grunting. He threw a clumsy blow with his open hand that caught Royce on the side of the head. Royce went back against the wall as though he had been hit with a crowbar. He tried to brace himself. Russell came in low, using his head like a battering ram.

Royce felt the white fire of anger. He sensed his strength coming back to him, flowing into him like burning oil.

He had come too far to louse it up now.

"Okay, friend," he whispered. "Let's see how good a job they did on you."

Royce attacked, protecting himself with his arms. He was bigger than Russell and he used his reach. He backed Russell across the room, hurting him.

Lead with your left, stupid, he told himself.

He did. He threw no more wild roundhouse punches. He jabbed with his left, keeping it in Russell's face. Russell was awkward; he could not counter. Russell's nose started to bleed. Royce used his right sparingly, going for the eyes.

Russell backed against the table. He groped for a wooden chair, lifted it over his head.

Royce went in under it. He drove a left to the belly, folding Russell like an accordion. The chair crashed to the floor. Royce swung a short right uppercut, straightening him up again.

Russell was helpless. He was a target, nothing more.

Royce took his time. He threw a left with all his strength behind it. Russell started down, his eyes glassy, his arms jerking spasmodically. Royce clipped him with a right as he fell.

Royce got on top of him. He took Russell's head in both hands, grabbing it by the long black hair. He raised the head to slam it against the hard tile floor.

He stopped before he completed the action. His anger drained away. Russell was completely helpless. That head he held in his hands harbored a brain. It might not be Russell's brain any longer, but still . . .

He lowered the head gently to the floor and staggered to his feet. He recovered his rifle and sank into a chair. He began to shake and his chest heaved. He felt sick at his stomach.

Where were the baboon-things? If they had not noticed all the racket in the house they must be deaf. Or else . . .

He looked at the beaten body on the floor.

"Jesus, Bob," he said in a low voice. "I didn't mean. . ."

The body stirred. The bloodshot eyes opened and looked right at him.

"Royce?"

It was the voice of Bob Russell.

Royce crossed over to him, his heart hammering. He knelt down and cradled Russell's head in his arm. "Bob, can you hear me?"

The sick smell of the man was overpowering. The eyes were filmed, distant. "Hear you," he said weakly.

"What's happened? What can I do?"

There was a silence that seemed long. Royce was afraid that Russell was . . . gone again. Then he heard the whispered words: "Kill me."

Royce, who had been on the verge of doing exactly that a few minutes earlier, groped for something to say. "Tell me what happened."

"Hard . . . to talk. Can't most of time. Am caught . . . inside. Can't explain. *It* will be back. You don't understand." The voice faded away.

"Bob, listen to me. I know about them. I know about the ship and the baboons. Did they take you to the ship? What are they after? What did they do to you?"

The eyes stared at him. The bloody face frowned in desperate concentration. "Came . . . before rains. Round metal, spider legs. Can't remember . . . things. Lights. Noise. Something . . . inside me. In my head. But all crazy, confused. Didn't work, Royce. They don't . . . know enough yet. Not even for baboons. They . . . it . . . so different. . . ."

"*What do they want?*"

"Don't know. They're afraid. So different. Can't explain. Don't understand us, this world. My head . . . it's *coming back*. Don't let it. Kill me. Don't let it come back. . . ."

Royce stood up, backed away. He had no guidelines by which he could act. He held his rifle ready and did nothing.

Russell's body twitched on the red tile floor. A groan of pain and despair was wrenched from the lips of the beaten face. The eyes opened wide. Strange eyes—seeing and not seeing, mirrors for an inner contest that had no name. The body got up on all fours, shuddered. The mouth whined. A foul, sick smell filled the room.

Royce watched in horror. The blows he had struck must have upset some delicate balance. If there were two . . . beings . . . in that body, he must have jolted one of them until it could not function. It was coming back, taking over, but it was hurt, crippled. . . .

Bob Russell's body crawled slowly into a corner of the room. One arm reached up, groped blindly at the wall. The arm fell back. The body collapsed. It trembled for a moment and was still.

Royce walked hesitantly over to the thing that had been a man. He knew the signs; he had seen enough of death to recognize it when it came. He felt for the pulse to be sure. There was no sign of life. He forced himself to look at the face. He was hoping for some sign of peace, of calm, but he saw only agony.

Did I kill him . . . them? Was I responsible?

He sensed the room around him. The striped zebra-skin throw rugs, the kudu head, the cold massive fireplace. The pictures of Russell's wife and sons. The shelves of books. The African masks. The tall old grandfather clock, no longer ticking away the seconds of eternity.

It had been a good house. A happy and solid and productive house.

"I'm sorry," Royce said aloud. "I would have done better if I could."

He did not even consider trying to bury Bob Russell.

There was no time for that, and perhaps Bob would have preferred to stay where he was. He picked the body up and put it on the couch.

Without hope, he walked into the hallway. The telephone was set into a niche about halfway to the bedroom. He did not turn on a light. He picked up the phone, lifted the receiver. The phone was dead.

Royce felt nothing at all; he was beyond disappointment. He went on into the bedroom, got a blanket, and covered Russell's body.

Numbly, he walked back to the kitchen. He opened the refrigerator, found some cheese that had not spoiled. He forced himself to eat it. He drank two glasses of water.

There was nothing more that he could do. He had failed, and more than failed. *They* had taken over Bob Russell, a human being. And he had left Kathy and the children at the Baboonery.

He could not get to Mitaboni. The river crossed the road about a mile from Russell's place and he could not cross it. He could only go back.

If he could make it. . . .

If there was anything to go back to. . . .

Wait a minute.

"The car," he whispered. "Bob had a car."

He went outside through the kitchen door, his rifle ready in his hands. He flattened himself against the wall of the house, letting his eyes adjust to the starlight. He saw no sign of the baboon-things. He believed that they were all so sick that they would not be dangerous, but he took

no chances. He moved silently around the house. The
night was very still.

He eased his way past the long line of the front porch
and paused at the corner. He studied the outbuilding that
Russell had used as a garage. The building was dark and
silent.

Royce moved in a crouching run to the outbuilding,
his boots sucking at the mud. There was no door. He
slipped inside and almost collided with Russell's Land
Rover. He worked the catch on the door and slid under the
wheel. The door made a loud click when he closed it.

His fingers explored the ignition switch. The keys
were not there. He remembered that Russell had once told
him that he kept the keys in the vehicle, but he had not
mentioned exactly where. He tried the panel that ran
along the dashboard and found nothing. He checked the
sunshades. Nothing but dust. There was very little space
under a Land Rover seat, but he tried that, too. Nothing.

Royce forced himself not to panic. It was incredible
that the baboon-things had not bothered him. Russell, of
course, had been controlled from inside; he required no
guards. But the baboons must have heard the racket in the
house, and they must have seen him. The only possible
explanation was that the baboons were not able to function
properly. Royce knew that a wild baboon removed from its
troop could not survive. It must be still worse for *these*
baboons: robbed even of their natural behavior patterns,
manipulated by an alien intelligence that had not yet
learned to cope with a strange world. . . .

Royce twisted in the seat. There were storage compartments lining both sides of the back. He tried the one immediately behind him. His searching fingers closed on two keys strung on a sturdy clasp chain.

A wave of relief almost made him giddy. If he could get the damned thing going . . .

He switched on the ignition and waited a long minute. He jabbed the floor starter with his slippery boot. The engine whined, sputtered, and died. No matter: the battery was okay. He tried it again and the engine caught. He gave it some gas. The roar of the engine blasted at his ears.

Royce set the knobbed lever in the four-wheel mud drive and backed the Land Rover out of the building. He turned on the lights; there was no point to driving in the dark with all the noise he was making. He turned the vehicle carefully and got it headed down the road. He picked up speed. The Land Rover slipped a little from side to side but it was not serious. He drove through the rows of dark sisal without incident.

He bumped out onto the paved main road and turned to the left. The road was in poor condition and the chuckholes and puddles of standing water forced him to take it easy. Nevertheless, it was a breeze compared to walking. There was no obstacle that could stop a Land Rover and he could almost relax as he drove.

He kept going until the beams of his headlights glinted on the river of rushing flood water that had washed out the road. He pulled over and stopped. The water level had dropped some, but the ditch of fast water was still a good twenty-five yards across. He turned off the ignition, cut the lights, and climbed out.

The easy part was over. He would have to walk again.

He gave himself no time to think. He plunged into the brush and picked his way to the bank of the swollen stream. He had more clearance now that the water had receded, and he was able to trudge through the mud at a fairly good clip. He did not need his flashlight. The scattered stars were clear and a warm yellow moon shone through rips in the clouds. There was no threat of rain.

Royce found his rope without difficulty and crossed the swift water. It was much easier this time. He sloshed back to the main road and headed for the Baboonery turnoff.

He walked as though in a trance, just concentrating on moving one heavy boot after the other. The stars turned above him and the moon faded to silver. He heard the calls of a few night birds from the wet black trees; once a leopard coughed from the bush on his left.

When Royce scrambled across the erosion ditch and started down the Baboonery road, it was almost four o'clock in the morning. His neck was sore and his shoulders were stiff. A muscle twitched maddeningly under his left eye. His legs were like iron posts. He kept going by setting himself a series of attainable goals: that baobab tree, that puddle, that rock.

He made it to his waiting Land Rover and stared at it almost without recognition. He climbed in and got underway. He drove clumsily at first with his numbed arms and legs. After he nearly got stuck in the mud, he forced himself to concentrate on what he was doing.

It was daylight when the vehicle jolted across the

railroad tracks. A fat golden sun was floating up into a blue sky that harbored islands of dark-bottomed white clouds. The rain-sodden world seemed to be holding its breath.

When Royce pulled up beside the main building, he had been gone a little more than twenty-four hours.

He climbed out of the mud-spattered Land Rover. He did not even have time to look around.

The door opened and Kathy ran out.

As soon as he saw her, he knew that he was too late.

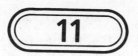

11

ROYCE TOOK HIS wife in his arms. He could feel the tense trembling of her body. He held her tightly, trying to reassure her with a strength that almost failed him. The words they did not speak were the most important words of all. They said: *We're alive, you and I. We're not hurt. Whatever has happened, we're not licked yet.*

Kathy pushed him back finally. She held both of his hands in hers. She smiled a little, her tired eyes wet with tears. "You look terrible. I'm so glad to see you."

"I've seen you looking better yourself. You've been up all night, haven't you? What in the hell happened?"

She did not answer him directly. "Bob Russell? The telephone? Is help coming?"

"I'm afraid we're still alone in this, sugar. My big rescue mission was a bust." Quickly, as undramatically as he could, he told her what had happened. "But what went on *here*?"

163

Kathy took a deep breath, searching for coherent words. She shook her head. "You better . . . see it first."

She led him toward the shed that housed the generator. Even from a distance the damage was obvious. The flimsy structure had been ripped to shreds. The drainage ditches were still intact, but their purpose no longer existed. The generator was wrecked. Royce took one look at what was now a pile of junk and knew that it was hopeless. He had repaired that cantankerous generator more times than he cared to remember, but his efforts had amounted to little more than inspired tinkering. He was not enough of a mechanic to rebuild a demolished generator from the ground up. In any case, he did not have the necessary equipment. The generator was finished and it would *stay* finished.

Tired as he was, the significance of the destroyed generator could not escape him. They had no lights except for a couple of camp lanterns. The freezers were out, which threatened their food supply. The pump would not function, but water at least was no immediate problem.

He thought: *They may have trouble with baboon behavior patterns, to say nothing of human behavior patterns. But they can damn well figure out a primitive electrical system. And they can set us up for a long, long night. . . .*

"What else?" he said.

Kathy took him to the long-roofed baboon shelter. Six of the cages had been broken into. Six baboons were gone.

"I guess they needed some replacements," Royce said

in what he hoped was a light tone. "The troops are getting a little thin."

"They waited until late. It must have been nearly midnight," Kathy said wearily. (*Midnight*, Royce thought. *Where was I at midnight? I must have been just about leaving Bob Russell's—could that have been just last night?*) "They knew what they were after—knew just where to go. They probably knew you were gone. They headed straight for the generator and the cages. The men heard them, saw them. They did what they could. They drove them off with bows and arrows. Mutisya was bitten in the leg. I cleaned it up, bandaged it. The men are afraid, Royce. They don't know what is going on. I can't even begin to explain. And *I'm* afraid. All those hours . . . no lights . . . not knowing if they were coming back. . . . The kids don't understand at all; they're so damned *cheerful*. . . ."

Kathy's voice was rising, veering toward hysteria. Royce cut her off. "The things that came . . . just baboons?"

"They're *not* just baboons. You know . . ."

"I mean, just in baboon form? Nothing else? No machines, no armor, no men?"

"I—we—just saw baboons. Royce, what are we going to *do*? I can't face another night here in the dark. I'm only human, I'm scared, I've got Susan and Barbara to think about. I'll do anything you say, but we can't just *sit* here."

Only human. I'm only human, too. Is that enough?

"Look, Kathy. I'm dead on my feet. I can't even think. I'm here and we'll be ready for them tonight. But I won't be of any use if I'm a walking zombie. Tell Wathome to rustle up some breakfast. I want to talk to Elijah and Mutisya. It isn't too likely that anything big will happen before it gets dark. I've got to get a few hours of sleep—you should too. Then we'll figure out what we can do."

Tears rose in Kathy's eyes again. She had hoped—believed—that help was on the way, that the nightmare would be over with his return. All through that terrible night she had kept herself going by holding fast to the thought that Royce would be back with the sun, that Royce would somehow take care of things. And now he was back, and it was all as it was before. . . .

He held her, tried to comfort her. "Baby, we'll be okay. We can all get in the Land Rover if we have to. We can drive to a place where they can never find us." *(And where might that be, friend? At the bottom of a mudhole?)* "As our British friends say, you've got to keep your pecker up."

The phrase always tickled Kathy; she managed a feeble smile. "That's a hell of a thing to say to a woman."

"It refers, I think, to a bird's beak. Anyhow, you've got to trust me. I'm all there is."

She kissed him lightly. "I guess you'll have to do, then. Sorry to go all female on you. I'll get Wathome busy in the kitchen."

She left him and Royce almost staggered with the release from play-acting. He was so shot he could barely stand. His hopes, too, had gone down the drain. He saw no way out, no effective action he could take.

Unless . . .

There was some truth, perhaps, in the old adage: *The best defense is a good offense.* He had been on the defensive from the beginning. If he could hit them where they lived . . .

Yeah, but *what* offense? Bows and arrows?

He rubbed his burning eyes. His head felt as though it were stuffed with cotton. It was dangerous to try to make plans now, he knew. He just wasn't tracking.

He walked on rubber legs to the men's quarters. Mutisya got up out of bed to let him in. Royce embraced the man without awkwardness. "I know what you did last night," he said. "I thank you for it. Someday, I hope I can thank you properly."

Mutisya retained his dignity. "A man does what he must do," he said quietly. There was a gentle rebuke in his tone. Royce should not have been surprised, he seemed to be saying, that the men had done their jobs properly.

Royce examined Mutisya's leg by loosening the bandage. The puncture wounds from the spiked baboon canines were deep but clean. There was no sign of infection. "We'll want to change that dressing before tonight," he said, pulling the bandage tight again. "Is it painful?"

Mutisya grinned, exposing his filed teeth. "Compared to a Masai spear, it is nothing. I am well."

"Give it as much rest as you can. I have a job for Elijah, but I want you to stay off that leg for awhile. Okay?"

"Okay, Mr. Royce."

Royce found Elijah and expressed his thanks to him.

He told him to get a crew together and drag in some firewood. "Pile it in the places where the outside lights are," he said. "It will be better than nothing."

Elijah blinked behind his tinted glasses. "The wood is wet," he said with his customary optimism. "It will not burn."

"We have petrol—plenty of it now that we can't keep the generator going. The wood will burn."

Elijah looked dubious but Royce was too tired to argue. He plodded across the muddy ground with the welcome sun warm on his aching shoulders. He entered the breezeway, greeted Wathome who had a fire going in the cookstove, and slumped down at the wooden table in the sitting room.

"No place like home," he muttered.

He fought to stay awake until the food arrived, too weary even to attempt conversation with Kathy. He drank two cups of strong, black coffee, which had no effect on him whatsoever. He ate three fried eggs, six slices of fried Spam, and four pieces of charred toast. Surprisingly, it all tasted delicious.

He went into the familiar bedroom and felt better when he saw the kids still sound asleep. He moved to take a shower, remembered that there was no water, and simply piled into bed without any preamble. It felt great.

"Call me by three this afternoon," he muttered. "Don't forget, for God's sake."

Kathy smiled. "It's not likely to slip my mind," she said.

Royce buried his head in the pillows and closed his eyes.

Sleep was instantaneous.

When you get *really* tired, there are no thoughts at all.

"Royce!"

A detached part of him, floating way up near the surface, heard Kathy's voice. But it was far away, it could not reach the rest of him. If he could get down deep enough . . .

"Royce!"

He felt something digging into his shoulder. The whole bed seemed to be shaking. He swam up from somewhere, not without a flash of irritation. He opened his eyes.

"Look," he muttered. "What kind of a joint is this anyway? When I leave a call I don't mean . . ."

Kathy cut him off. "Royce, wake up, for God's sake!"

"I'm awake." He blinked. "What is it? What's . . ."

Kathy's fingers tightened on his shoulder. "Barbara! She's gone. They've taken Barbara!"

Royce jerked up in the bed, his eyes wide and staring. He looked in confusion at the window, saw the curtains blowing gently and the sunlight beyond. "It's still light. What time is it? They wouldn't . . ."

"Oh, wake up, wake up! They came . . . the baboon-things . . . just now. I was in the kitchen with Susan.

Barby wandered outside to play in the mud . . . I didn't see her at first . . . she was right outside the door. . . ."

He felt a cold horror. "You *saw* them take her?"

"I saw them. They grabbed her and ran. I could hear her crying. Royce, we've got to get her back before . . . before . . ."

Royce leaped out of bed, threw on his clothes, yanked on his muddy boots. He grabbed his .375 and shoved Kathy ahead of him into the breezeway. "Show me. Quickly now. Exactly where did they go?"

Kathy pointed a trembling finger. Royce's eyes followed the line of sight, across the open compound, beyond the baboon cages, to the dark line of the bush still rain-wet under the bright afternoon sun. He saw movement there, shadows. . . .

Royce was engulfed in an anger and a terror beyond anything he had ever known. He could face danger to himself with understanding if not with enthusiasm; he was a man, and he had years of experience behind him. But to seize a child, a little girl five years old, to carry her off into something she could not possibly comprehend. . . .

It was *his* failure, of course. Barby could not defend herself. And he had been *sleeping*.

Even through his sick fury, the questions insinuated themselves. Questions and answers. . . .

Why had they taken Barby? Obviously, because she *was* a child. They had learned something from Bob Russell, learned perhaps that they could not yet cope effectively with an adult. They had not been completely successful with the baboons. They might take Barby away with them, experiment with her, come back when they knew more. . . .

Why hadn't they waited for darkness, after going to the trouble of knocking out the generator? Well, they were not fools, whatever else they were. They had seen him come back. They knew he would have to sleep, knew he could be ready for a night attack. They were at least as intelligent as he was. They had simply revised their plans.

And now . . .

His hatred drowned out everything else. He could *see* them out there in the bush, moving, watching. . . .

He ran through the slow-drying mud beneath a deep-blue sky fragmented with drifting clouds still swollen with rain. He pulled up at the baboon cages, his heart hammering. He threw the heavy rifle to his shoulder, peered through the telescopic sight. He picked one of them up almost at once. His belly tightened as the cross-hairs centered on the olive-gray coat, the naked snout, the gleaming canines.

His finger curled on the trigger.

He did not fire.

Royce lowered the .375, his hands shaking. He swallowed hard to keep from vomiting.

Think, you fool. You've made enough mistakes. If you shoot every animal out there, what then? Will that get Barby back?

He looked more closely at those dark forms at the edge of the bush. What were they doing there? Why hadn't they gone with the others? Surely, they knew they were vulnerable if they did not run. What if they couldn't run? What if they were too sick, too weak to escape?

He had to get through to that ship, wherever it was. He had to get Barbara out of there. He couldn't storm it with a popgun and bows and arrows.

Whatever else he did, he had to get his girl *out*.

Royce spun around, shouting to Mutisya and Elijah. He sprinted to the lab storeroom, scooped up two bottles of sernyl. He filled the three pole-syringes he had. He hollered to Wathome to throw some maize and pineapple into the Land Rover and fill it with petrol.

With the rifle in one hand and the syringe in the other, he led the men on a dead run toward the creatures in the bush. He took no safety precautions. It was speed that counted now, nothing else.

The baboon-things saw him coming. There were four of them, all males. They coughed and snorted in fear. They tried to retreat into the tangle of the bush, but they could not run. They staggered and fell, saliva dripping from their snouts. Their eyes were cloudy and dull. The stink of sickness hovered over them like a preview of death.

The animals turned at bay. There was an alien intelligence in their primate skulls, but illness reduces all creatures to the same level. They functioned as sick and desperate beasts, nothing more.

They bared their fangs and waited.

Royce did not hesitate. He faked at the nearest one, drawing a weak lunge and a snapping of jaws. He leaped behind the animal and jabbed with his syringe. He hit him hard and rammed the plunger home.

The animal screamed, biting the air.

Royce backed away and refilled his syringe. Mutisya, despite his bad leg, already had another baboon cornered. Elijah, with the third syringe, was taking his own sweet time, protecting himself.

Royce stuck his second baboon, snatched the pole from Elijah, and went after the last animal. The baboon ignored his fake and attacked with a snarl of hate. Royce kicked him in the face with his boot, feeling a crunch of bone. He jabbed him in the belly with his needle, slammed the plunger with the heel of his hand, and leaped back.

He stood there, his chest heaving, sweat staining his shirt. The sernyl did its job. The baboons wobbled about on rubber legs, collapsed, twitched, and were still.

Royce eyed the thin bodies with a raging mixture of emotions: fear, anger, wonder, loathing, pity. . . .

"Watch them," he said to Mutisya.

His thoughts on his child somewhere out there in the waiting bush, he ran back to get the Land Rover.

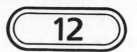

12

THE WARM AFTERNOON sun stroked the rain-soaked land with golden fingers. The air was still and heavy. It was hot enough for wisps of smoky vapor to rise from the sodden acacias. The washed gray bulges of the baobabs stood impassively in the sunlight, indifferent to either rain or sun. Insects buzzed in the flattened grass and squadrons of birds feasted until they could hardly fly.

The back road to Mitaboni, thick with choking dust the last time Royce had driven it when he had checked his traps an eternity ago, was a trail of mud. There were no wheel tracks ahead of the Land Rover; no vehicle had come this way since the rains had started. The two rails that paralled the road on the left had a thin patina of rust on them; no train had gotten through for a long, long time.

The slowing of the rains and the heat of the sun had helped to drain the road. It was not impossible now, at least on this side of the Tsavo. It was merely improbable.

175

The battered Land Rover was heavily loaded this time, which was both an advantage and a disadvantage. It did not skid and fishtail as it had done when Royce had driven it alone, but it dug into the soft spots more deeply and persistently. Royce had four men with him. Elijah and Wathome rode up front in the cab. He had taken Elijah so that he would not lose face with his men and Wathome because he was steady and reliable. Nzioki and Kisaluwa rode in the back with the unconscious baboons. They were both big strong men not unduly cursed with imagination. Whenever the Land Rover got stuck they vaulted over the side and pushed.

Royce had left Mutisya with Kathy and Susan. There was nothing else he could do, and in any case Mutisya was the best man for the job. He could not carry a load through the bush on his bad leg, but he could fight if he had to. Royce trusted him more than other man he knew in Kenya, white or black.

Royce tried not to think about Barbara. Whenever her image slipped into his mind his vision blurred and his thoughts went wild. He knew that he had to think clearly now, had to keep his emotions out of it. If he surrendered to hate, whatever small chance the child had was gone.

He fought the wheel, nursed the whining engine, picked his course his skill and care. He did not try to bull his way through the slop on the road. He stayed out of the ruts, took advantage of every patch of grass, every stretch of firm earth. . . .

He forced himself to think about *them*.

He knew about where they were. The location of the

eerie glow that he had seen was burned into his brain. It was this side of the roaring Tsavo River, thank God, off there to the right in the bush. He had gotten to within a mile of the source of that glow that long-ago night. He could have found it whenever he wished, even in the torrent of the rains. It would have been foolish before, perhaps suicidal. His chances were not good now. He knew that, but he had no other choice.

Would they know that he was not coming as an attacker bent on revenge? Would they even wait to see what his intentions were? If he ever got back to Kathy at all, would he still be Royce Crawford . . . or something else?

Well, he could always shoot himself if it came to that. And he could take a few of them with him, too. . . .

Don't think that way. Choke it off.

What about them, those beings waiting for him in the warm mists of a world not their own? Could they understand him any better than he understood them? Could he see himself through their eyes? He had to try. If he miscalculated their response to his actions. . . .

It came to him that he had never really seen them. A vapor trail in the sky, alien eyes staring from the skull of a baboon, a man who had once been Bob Russell, strange tracks in the African earth—these were their only visible signs. He could not imagine what they might look like. He supposed that it did not matter. They might be ugly or beautiful. They might produce no reaction at all. He might not even recognize them as living beings. It made no difference. It was what they *did* that counted. Octopus or dragon or blob of jelly—it was all the same.

He could not know what purpose had brought them to this world. He thought he knew why they had chosen this particular place; he could not believe that it had been an accident. This remote spot in the African bush must have seemed ideal from their point of view. They could operate with a minimum of interference and a maximum of safety. There were isolated human beings to observe, and there were simpler primates to experiment with—baboons that were enough like men so that men themselves used them for medical research. That was strategy, of course. It told him nothing about the nature of the game that was being played.

Royce knew one thing, at least. This was a dangerous world to them. They were running terrible risks. They were taking casualties. Whatever project they were engaged in, this was no picnic. They were vulnerable outside their ship. They were in a strange and hostile land. They must feel that they were surrounded by monsters, aliens bent on destroying them. They had killed, it was true, but perhaps they had only done so in what they regarded as self defense.

Suppose one day man landed on some distant planet. Why would *he* have come, what impulse would have driven him across the darkness and the light-years? Could he explain, and would he even try? If he set out to explore that fearful world, if he trapped some specimens, what would he do if he were attacked by monstrous beings he could not understand? Would he stay his hand, leave them in peace?

Royce knew with a hard cold certainty that the killing

had to stop. No matter who had made the first false move, the chain of fear and destruction had to be broken. A man does not worry about a world or two worlds when the life of his child is at stake. It was Barby he was fighting for. But if she were to have any chance at all, there had to be a new kind of contact between him and them.

Somehow, he had to show them that man could be a better ally than an enemy. He had to prove that he was more than a mindless savage. He had to demonstrate that a man could be a friend worth having. If *they* could not risk compassion, then *he* must take that first tough step.

If his gesture did not move them—if they were so different from man that they could not be moved—then he had lost. But he could not get his child back by firing at a spaceship with rifle bullets. He could not induce an act of mercy by more killing.

Royce ground his teeth together. The muscles of his arms stood out like taut ropes as he gripped the wheel. He did not know whether he was man enough for the job ahead. There was another side of him, a side that shrieked for vengeance, that wanted to surrender to hate, that wanted to cut loose and take the easy way. . . .

"Damn them," he whispered. "Damn them for coming here, damn them all."

He pushed the Land Rover as far as he could along the muddy trail, kept it going until the thunder of the flooded Tsavo was loud above the whine of the engine, and then jerked the wheel to the right. The vehicle jolted into the bush with a series of shuddering shocks. Royce engaged all four wheels but used his mud gear to maintain

speed. He could not bull his way through thick brush and
fallen trees, but it was surprising how much open country
there was in uncleared land. There were lanes of wet
brown grass and barren fields without a tree in them. The
ground was more uneven than the road, but thick mud was
less of a problem. He picked his course with care and he
made good progress. He had trailed many an animal this
way, and except for the jolts it was not particularly
difficult.

Royce pushed the Land Rover on for nearly twenty
minutes until the acacias and vines and thorny scrub brush
thickened around him. Shadows darkened the land and
the air grew still. A wall of damp vegetation confronted
him, and he knew that he would have to make a long and
time-consuming circle to get around it.

He stopped the Land Rover. There was a heavy silence in the air, broken only by the distant liquid roar of
the Tsavo. Mosquitoes and flies swarmed through the
open windows of the cab.

Royce leaped out, slapping at the bugs.

Now the fun starts, he thought.

It was a strange, slow procession that picked its hesi-
tant way through the darkening wilderness. The men
walked in single file, their footsteps cushioned by the
soggy ground. Royce went first, a limp baboon slung over
his left shoulder and a rifle in his right hand. Elijah
followed him, staggering under the weight of a folded tarp
and a canvas bag filled maize and pineapples. Royce
wanted Elijah right behind him; he knew that Elijah had

little stomach for this safari, and he needed to make certain that Elijah kept moving in the right direction. Nzioki and Kisaluwa came next, each carrying a baboon with something less than complete enthusiasm. Wathome brought up the rear with the last baboon and a sharp ax. Royce had confidence in Wathome, at least where cooking was not involved.

It was not, Royce thought, the most powerful possible assemblage to represent mankind in an encounter with an alien power. Perhaps, though, its very impotence constituted its best chance for success.

He forced his way forward, relying on his memory to take him in the right direction. There were no landmarks. He could feel the baboon stirring slightly on his shoulder. The dead weight dragged him down; it was like carrying a sixty-pound sack of lead. Insects bit his hands and face and he could do nothing to deter them. The clouds in the lowering sky grew thicker and blacker. If the rains came again . . .

He sensed what he could not see. He was getting closer to *them*. They were ahead of him. They must be very close now. He did not doubt that they were watching him somehow, waiting for him, sizing him up . . .

A brown flash bolted out of a clump of dead grass right in front of him. There was a snort of expelled air, a muted drumming of hooves pushing against the wet earth. Royce recognized the animal as a small bushbuck the instant he saw him, but his heart hammered so hard in his chest that he almost had to stop to catch his breath. He was keyed up so high that the slightest touch would have made him jump.

"Don't let it get dark yet," he whispered. "Don't let it rain." It might have been a prayer, though its target was uncertain. God, Mulungu, Allah, one of the local deities. . . .

He fought his way on. Thorns ripped at his legs. The pounding sound of the flooded river came clearly through the screening trees but Royce thought he heard a new sound now. A higher sound, steady but taut, a vibrant hum of tingling power. It was like the hot buzz of electricity in a high-tension line back home on a still day. . . .

He picked his way around a grotesquely swollen baobab tree, pushed through a curtain of clinging brush.

There it was, as he had always known it would be.

He stopped and stared.

It rested in the middle of a small clearing: white as new-fallen snow, smooth and featureless, terribly matter-of-fact and terribly *wrong* there in the confines of the African bush.

There was a cold white light coming from it, an aura that ignored the earthly shadows. The hum seemed louder and Royce almost thought he could see the thing move silently. It was *on*.

It was perfectly round, a great white globe. It looked like it could roll. It seemed to be resting on the ground but it made no impression at all, as though it were weightless. The blank smooth surface of the sphere looked more like plastic than metal. No, not plastic. Like a gigantic glowing white marble. . . .

It was hard to grasp the size of the thing. The mind

tried to find a slot to put it in, tried to check it against
something known, and the mind failed. It was big, yes, but
that was a pitiful word, an inadequate word. Mountains
are big, oceans are big, men are big. It was not as big as
the great rockets that men launched from this world—but
it was far larger than the capsules that perched on top of
those rockets. The thing was perhaps eighty feet across,
perhaps more. The size of a house with rooms higher than
any house, a vast shining bubble that moved through the
dark seas between worlds and stars. . . .

Royce thought: *Barby is in that thing. She has to be in
there. She's in there with them, whatever they are.*

The men crowded in behind him, staring with more
curiosity and fear than astonishment. They had seen so
many astounding things in their lifetimes, things that had
suddenly appeared in their world from outside—trains and
planes and trucks that growled along the dusty roads. They
were willing to accept anything now. They did not even
ask questions, fearing to be thought ignorant. They simply
waited for instructions.

Royce knew that he was close to death. He was certain
that the beings in that ship could wipe him out as easily as
he could step on a spider.

Act, he told himself. *They are waiting to see what we
are going to do. Show them.*

He lowered the twitching baboon to the ground, gently. He took the ax from Wathome and told the men to
remain as still as possible. He searched around in the
brush, not venturing any closer to the sphere. He found
some wood and hacked out six crude but sturdy poles. He

fashioned a rough point on one end of each pole and chopped a notch in the other end. The sound of the ax blade biting into the damp wood worried him, but he knew that his fear was irrational. *They* would know that the men had arrived. It would serve no purpose to aim at concealment.

He gathered up the poles and returned to the waiting Africans. "Okay," he said. "Leave the baboons. Bring the tarp. Wathome, stay with the baboons. Holler if they come to enough to move away. Quickly, now."

He moved out into the clearing. He forced himself to walk toward the glowing white sphere. He went to within thirty yards of it. He could *feel* the thing as it towered over him. The humming tension that surrounded it was a palpable force that made his skin crawl.

Royce tried not to think, tried to shut off his imagination. He did not look at the snowy monstrous bubble that rested so lightly on the alien earth. He spread out the greasy tarp and arranged the poles at the four corners and the two canvas side loops. One by one, he drove the pointed supports into the yielding ground with the blunt end of the ax head.

The men hoisted the tarp up into position and tied it to the notched poles with the short ropes that were already fastened to the tarp. The heavy canvas sagged a little but the structure held. The tarp was only some four feet off the ground.

Royce went back and got the bag of food from Wathome. He walked around the shelter so that he was in plain view from the blandly featureless sphere. He took the maize cobs and the pineapples from the canvas container, holding them up so they could be seen. He placed the food under the tarp.

"Now," he said, trying to speak in a normal tone of voice. "Bring the baboons. Put them in there under the tarp. Be very careful with them. Don't just *dump* them, understand?"

They got the baboons. All of them were awake now but still confused from the drug. The men handled them gingerly. Royce had a bad moment when the animal he was carrying twisted in his arms and tried to bite him. He was determined to just let the creature bite if he had to, but the baboon-thing was too weak and fuzzy-minded to press home his attack. They placed the twitching animals under the tarp, their heads toward the food.

"Okay," Royce said. "Back to the edge of the clearing there. Don't run. Take it easy. Just walk."

The men withdrew, leaving the crude gray shelter with its strange occupants. The pole-supported tarp stood there in the field, a homely and somehow pitiful contrast to the massive glowing sphere that dominated the earth.

Royce turned to face the Africans. He felt himself trembling with relief. He did not dare to hope yet, but at least no new disaster had struck. He knew that he had been responsible for bringing these men here, and it was not really their fight. It was *his* child that was in that thing.

"*Asante sana,*" he said. "Thank you. I won't forget your help. There may be danger here; I don't know. There is no need for you to stay. Go on back and help Mutisya.

Tell Mrs. Crawford that I am well and that everything is being done that can be done. Leave me the Land Rover. If you go now, you can reach the road before dark."

Elijah needed no urging. He adjusted his tinted glasses and struck off through the bush without a backward glance. Nzioki and Kisaluwa hesitated only a moment and followed the headman.

Wathome managed a tired smile. "I will stay if you wish," he said. "Miss Barbara was a friend to me."

Royce felt a stinging in his eyes. Mutisya, Wathome—they were good men. They had resources that he had not expected. He hated the barriers between them. Their differences were small indeed. Skin color, background, wealth—what did they matter in the perspective of that alien sphere from the depths of space? Men were men, that was all. "If you could help, my friend, I would ask you to stay." Royce tried to explain, tried to avoid the patronizing words of a *bwana* to a workman. "I am hoping that the . . . the people who have taken Barbara will let her go. If they do, I will bring her home. There is nothing to do but wait. If they don't let her go, I don't know what will happen. You have a family of your own. I think it is my responsibility to stay here. I think it is yours to go back where it may be safer."

Wathome nodded. He seemed neither glad nor sorry. He turned and followed the others on the backtrail through the bush.

Royce was alone.

13

THE AFRICAN NIGHT fell swiftly. It was as though the sea of thick black clouds had fallen from the sky, shrouding the earth. The air was very damp and Royce shivered in the sudden chill. There were no stars; there was not even a faint luminescence where the moon should be.

A wall of darkness pressed in behind him, a living darkness that stirred with padded footfalls and called with the soft songs of night birds. It was a darkness that seemed to stretch away unbroken to the shores of the Indian Ocean where silver-crested waves washed over the clean white sands. Royce could feel that darkness, but it did not concern him.

He stood at the edge of the clearing, his eyes fixed on the great glowing sphere. He could see no change in it. In the cold radiance of its own steady light it was bland and uncaring, a huge egg of white marble that might have been deposited on the earth by some monstrous bird.

There was no sign of activity, no alteration in the pitch of the taut humming that came from somewhere within its depths. It did nothing at all.

He could see the shelter clearly in the eerie glow. The baboon-things were still there; he could see their dark shadows beneath the tarp. The sernyl had long since worn off, of course. Royce figured that the creatures were so sick and weak that they could not move without great effort. In any case, they could probably not enter the ship unaided. Unless there was an atmosphere lock of some kind, they could not go into that alien interior without protection. Something would have to come out and get them. . . .

Royce stood for what seemed an eternity, hardly daring to move. He had rested his rifle against a tree. He stood far enough out into the open to show that his hands were empty.

A light rain began to fall. It was just enough to be visible against the cold glow of the sphere. Royce fancied that he could hear it ticking against the surface of the tarp. The muted rush of the Tsavo seemed louder to him, but that was surely his imagination.

He trembled a little, colder inside than out. Unless he had made a terrible mistake, he was no more than seventy yards from his daughter. Not even the length of a football field. He could run to her in eight or nine seconds if he could just get inside that thing. . . .

He could not shut off his mind forever. Barbara might already be dead. She might have been altered so that another mind was cradled inside her skull. *They* might be working on her even now, probing that small body that had known only a few short years, that had never known terror. . . .

Royce cursed silently but viciously. He cursed *them* and he cursed himself. He had made too many mistakes. If he had acted differently, if he had made the right moves, she would not be in there now. He would not be standing here like a fool in the night and the rain, helpless and afraid.

Come on, come on. Do something. Do anything.

He could get his rifle. He could advance into that unearthly glow. He could threaten the baboon-things under that tarp. He could drag one out into the light and put a bullet through that implanted brain behind the animal eyes.

And then—what?

He did not move. He forced himself to stay where he was. He could not afford the luxury of action.

He looked at his watch. It was only ten o'clock.

He groaned aloud. There was nothing he could do, nothing.

He waited between the living darkness and the cold white light of the machine.

It was nearly midnight and the rain was pattering down in heavier drops when the frozen tableau suddenly changed. The change was minor at first, but it was startling in a scene that had been utterly without motion for so long.

Royce held his breath, staring. His knees were so weak that he almost fell.

In the exact center of the surface of the glowing sphere, there was an alteration in the intensity of the cold white light. A circular area about ten feet across shifted from marble white to a dull solid gray. It changed again, seeming to flow from one texture to another. It turned to a metallic glistening black that was sharply outlined against the featureless surrounding white.

It moved.

It bulged outward, a black swelling on the smooth white sphere. A circular black column descended from the bubble. The shaft came down without a sound, seeming to materialize out of the very air. It touched the earth.

The bottom of the column went from jet black to the dull gray that Royce had seen a moment before. For a long minute, nothing happened.

Then, abruptly, there was an opening. There was nothing that opened like a door or a hatch. What had been solid was simply transformed into a space that led inside. A cold greenish light spilled like smoke out into the rain.

Something emerged from the column into the clearing.

Royce stood his ground, afraid to move and afraid not to move. The thing that had come out of the ship looked like a strange fat shining worm with legs. It seemed too large to have come out of the shaft. Its swollen, flexible body shimmered with white light. The light was intense; it hurt Royce's eyes. There were six legs: strong jointed black metallic appendages that blurred where they articulated with the serpentine body. The thing looked cumbersome and poorly designed, but it worked with fluid ease. The legs left sharp round depressions in the damp earth but they did not stick. The shining white body moved above the legs almost independently. Perhaps, Royce thought, the legs were not supports at all but served some other function. . . .

The thing was obviously not alive. It was a machine of some sort, a shell, a container that held life forms that Royce could not even imagine.

He *knew* that the thing was not empty.

The glaring white caterpillar flowed with an improbable grace through the rain. It gave off a crackling buzzing sound, different from the hum of the looming sphere. It crossed the space to the crude tarp shelter and stopped.

The fat worm's head seemed to grow longer. It dipped down and probed under the tarp like the questing trunk of an elephant. The shimmering white light illuminated the waiting baboon creatures as though a flare had been stuck in the soft earth.

There was a slow leakage of smoky cloudiness, a blurring of light and form. The four baboons remained motionless. The smudge of smoke-blue vapor surrounded the animals, obscuring them. The baboon-things were *absorbed*.

The cloudiness disappeared. The head of the shining caterpillar shrank to its former size and lifted in the wet air. The swollen sinuous body turned with precision and flowed back to the sphere, buzzing loudly. It seemed to coil into the cold green light that spilled from the bottom of the black shaft. The green light . . . stopped. The foot of the column went back to a dull solid gray.

The shelter was empty. There was nothing under the tarp.

The only sounds were the taut humming of the sphere, the distant roar of the Tsavo, and the gentle splashing of the falling rain. It seemed much darker despite the white glow of the sphere.

Royce stood in an agony of fear and indecision. He had played his only card. He had made the only move that was open to him. He had gambled on the psychology of the beings in that ship, hoping against hope that they were not as totally alien as they seemed.

If he had thrown away Barby's last chance . . .

If that glistening black column were withdrawn . . .

He swallowed hard. "Come on, come on, come on," he whispered.

It seemed to him that hours passed with that great white sphere resting impassively in the clearing. His watch told him that it had been only ten minutes.

The gray area at the bottom of the shaft . . . disappeared. Smoky green light eddied out into the rain. The shaft was open again.

Royce's hands were wet with sweat. He could feel cold icy drops dripping from beneath his arms. His heart thudded against his chest with a force that made him sway. He crossed his slippery fingers.

The shining worm-thing came out again, buzzing and clicking. It looked smaller now. It wound its way above its six-legged frame back to the shelter. The swollen head stretched down beneath the sagging tarp. The light almost blinded Royce but he kept his eyes riveted on it. The blurring vapor swirled like blue smoke. He could not see what was happening.

The head withdrew. The strangely graceful caterpillar made no attempt to approach Royce. It turned in a blaze of white light and went back to the sphere. The opening filled in behind it, shutting off the smoky green light. The dull gray color of the bottom of the column shifted to a jet black. The black shaft lifted without a sound into the air, seeming to flow upward into the dark bubble in the center of the glowing sphere. The swelling on the smooth globe collapsed and was gone. The circular area where the bubble had been went from metallic black to dull gray to marble white.

The sphere was as it had been: bland, featureless, an uncaring egg resting on the alien earth.

Royce moved. He could not wait any longer. He walked slowly out into the clearing. He felt the cool raindrops on his face, the ache in his stiff legs, the yielding softness of the wet turf. He kept his eyes fixed on the small, lonely shelter. He thought he could see something under the water-heavy tarp, something still and motionless. . . .

There was no visible reaction from the white sphere.

He ducked under the edge of the tarp, crawled into the shelter on his hands and knees. The animal smell of the baboons was very strong. There was another smell, too: an acrid oily smell that suffused the close air.

The shelter was not empty. There was a form, a bundle, curled up on the flattened grass.

Royce touched it, feeling dry cloth and warm flesh

underneath. He turned it over, gently. He stared at a pale drawn face, close-cropped hair, a small still body dressed in wrinkled blue jeans and a smudged yellow T-shirt.

"Barby," he whispered. "Barby, honey."

The child stirred at his touch, shivered. She opened her eyes. They seemed blank at first, disoriented. Royce felt a chill of terror when he saw those eyes. But the eyes cleared. There was recognition.

She reached out for him.

"Daddy?" she said weakly. "Daddy?"

Royce scooped her up, pressed her to him. "Everything is okay," he whispered. "Hang on now."

He lunged out from under the shelter, his child in his arms.

He ran.

Royce never knew how he got through the dark and dripping bush. He did it mindlessly, never stopping, never hesitating. He made no false moves. He did not give a thought to snakes or wild animals, despite the fact that he had left his rifle back at the edge of the clearing. He simply clutched his child tightly to him and *ran*.

The Land Rover was waiting. He put Barby in the seat next to him, her eyes wide with excitement now. He kicked the engine into life and churned the vehicle through the trail he had made, following the tracks of his wheels. The path was clear in the bright headlight beams. It was still raining, but the rain had not been hard enough to make new mud a problem.

He skidded out onto the road, spun to the left, and

gave it some gas. The tires took hold. The Land Rover whipped and jolted between dark lanes of dripping vegetation. Barby held on tightly to the gray metal shelf that stretched under the instrument panel. Her small body bounced alarmingly on the lightly padded seat but Royce was not about to slow down now. He shouted encouragement and maintained all the speed he dared.

He saw the welcome lights of the Baboonery at last. The men had lit the fires and kept them going somehow. There were paraffin lamps gleaming through the windows.

Royce hit the horn in sheer exuberance. The Land Rover skidded to a stop. There was a sudden silence as he cut the engine. He jerked open the door and almost fell in his haste to get out.

"It's okay!" he yelled into the shadows. "I've got her! Everything is okay!"

Figures, running figures. Laughter, that wonderful long-absent sound. Clutching hands. Faces: Mutisya, Mbali, Wathome, Kathy, Susan. . . .

Kathy almost smothered Barbara as she lifted the child from the Land Rover. Tears were streaming down her haggard face. Susan jumped up and down, half with glee at her sister's return and half in annoyance at being left out of things.

"We don't have any electricity," Susan said, yanking on Barbara's arm. "We don't have any water."

"A baboon almost ate me," Barby said solemnly, topping Susan's best effort.

Royce started to follow his family through the breezeway door and then stopped when he felt a touch on his shoulder. He turned.

"Mr. Royce," Wathome said, pointing. "Look!"

He could not miss it; it filled the sky. Back there where he had been, back there in the dark bush between the Mitaboni road and the lost and lonely Tsavo, an intense white light pulsed upward through the blackness and the rain. It grew brighter still as he watched, a miniature sun that transformed night into day.

He could hear it now: a taut throbbing hum that stirred like a keening alien wind out of that distant clearing and whined through the swollen baobabs and the dripping branches of the acacia trees.

He called out to Kathy and she came to stand by his side. He wanted to say something, but no words came. There were no words. They were witnesses to an event that had no parallel on the earth, an ending or a beginning. . . .

He took her hand, knowing that it was a childish gesture. He felt small and powerless and he reached out for comfort, for warmth, for reassurance.

The white light seemed to explode. There was a dull and muffled report, not unlke the detonation of a few sticks of dynamite deep underground. A wave of warm air touched his face and was gone. The explosion of white light . . . vanished.

There was a whistling roar and an arc of silver mounted into the sky on a column of thunder. The sound was gone in an instant. A silver glow lingered briefly beneath the torn clouds and then it, too, was gone.

There was only the great night and the feeble fires that man had made.

Royce felt a curious mixture of weariness and exultation, joy and a kind of sadness. The tension that had filled him for so long drained away. He felt an unutterable relief, a sense of triumph, a strange awareness of loss.

"They're gone," he said softly. "Whoever they were, whatever they wanted, they're gone."

And the dark world around him, no longer threatening, seemed to stir and rustle and murmur in the gentle rain that fell from a known and familiar sky: *gone, gone, gone. . .*

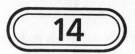

14

T HE RAINS WERE over. There would be no more rain
in Kenya for many months. The golden African sun
blazed in a vast and cloudless blue sky. The swollen brown
rivers retreated from the ravaged floodplains and flowed
clean and fresh between shattered banks. Standing water
was absorbed into the earth, finally, and the trails of mud
dried and cracked with long fissure lines.

The land was reborn in a miraculous and astonishing
burst of life. Green was everywhere: a crisp new green that
soothed the eye and refreshed the mind. The bush, once a
barren world of dry gray-brown branches and dead grass
and blowing red dust, was a riot of living things. It was a
new earth, a different earth. Rain in an arid land had done
its age-old work, touching seeds long dormant, patiently
waiting grass, questing roots, budding leaves . . .

The vegetation was taller than a man and so thick that
Royce could not see through it. Even the baobabs were
lush and green. The cactuslike euphorbia seemed to grow

before his eyes. The convolvulus had sprouted into clumps that were eight and nine feet high, and the plants were covered with white blossoms that looked like morning glories. Bees droned in the warm, still air.

The toy whistles of the busy trains were heard again and the rust stains were ground from the gleaming tracks by heavy wheels of steel. Crews of sweating men worked on the roads. Bridges were rebuilt across deceptively gentle streams. In time, even the red dust came back again to settle on wax-green leaves and the tough pitted hides of rhino and elephant.

The main road was open, to Nairobi and beyond.

It was all as it had once been, and yet for Royce it could never be the same.

The generator was repaired with monumental labor and minimal cost and the Baboonery lights came on again in the black velvet of the African night. The staccato sounds of drumming came once more from dances near the station. Piles of supplies were unloaded from the Nairobi train. Matt Donaldson came back to supervise the repairs to his battered safari camp.

Royce tried to pick up the threads of his life. It was a curious life certainly—he saw it now as though through alien eyes—but nonetheless he had a job to do. He was not a man to quit without warning; he would do what he had to do until he could be replaced. He owed that, at least, to the Africans who worked for him; if the Baboonery operation collapsed, they might all be fired. He did not regard his decision as being in any way heroic. The threat was over, after all. There was no point in scurrying for safety on a retroactive basis.

He set his traps, caged his animals. He resumed the shipments of baboons to the United States. He told himself that what he was doing was good and valuable. He tried to remember the benefits that would come from medical research. It was not easy.

Royce was not fond of baboons. Certainly, he did not idealize them. But the parallels were too close; they made him feel guilty and uncomfortable. *They*, too, had taken baboons, experimented with them, used them for purposes that had seemed worthwhile to *them*. *They* had done it for the same reason that Royce was doing it: the baboons were a lot like human beings. There was a kinship there. Perhaps there was also a responsibility. . . .

And he looked closely at every baboon he trapped. He looked for signs of weakness, of sickness, of an alien intelligence staring out through desperate primate eyes. Not all of the transformed baboons could have made it back to the ship. He doubted that any of them had survived, but how could he be sure? Were any of them still out there in the bush, bewildered and alone, stranded voyagers in a world not their own?

No, he could not ever again see a baboon without wondering, without remembering. . . .

He wrote to Ben Wallace in Houston, asking that a replacement be sent. He gave reasons, but not the real ones. He told about the fire and the floods and said that his family wanted to leave, which was true enough. He detailed the fine work that had been done by the men and recommended raises for all of them. In particular, he singled out Mutisya and Wathome. He suggested that Mutisya be given enough training so that one day he could manage the Baboonery himself. He made no attempt to tell Wallace the true story of what had happened. Houston was far, far away in another world, and Ben Wallace was only a man.

Royce returned several times to the place where the great white sphere had been. It would have been fitting, he thought, if no grass had grown in that lonely clearing. It should have been marked somehow; it should have carried the imprint of the strange visitation it had known. But the grass grew there as everywhere, and the flowers nodded in the sun, and the warm wind rustled through the leaves.

They had come and they had gone, and they had left no sign upon the land.

Royce had taken no photographs. He had been fighting for survival, and picture-taking had never crossed his mind. In any case, he knew, photographs would prove nothing. Pictures could always be faked.

The bodies of the baboon-things he had stored in the freezer had decomposed in the weeks before the power from the generator had been restored; they were only stinking chunks of decaying meat. He had buried the bodies without attempting an autopsy.

Bob Russell's corpse had been found in his house, still on the couch where Royce had placed it. Royce read the obituary in the *East African Standard* that came in on the train. The death was ascribed to natural causes. Russell's death had created no special stir. He had not been the only man to perish in the isolation and confusion of the floods.

Royce had not the slightest desire to live out his life as a freak, and he was not anxious to get involved with the Kenya Police. No action of his could help Bob Russell now. He knew that Russell would not have held him responsible for his death. He would probably have agreed that there were some things better left unsaid.

Royce knew, too, what would happen if he tried to tell his story, the story of what had really happened during those strange days and nights at the Baboonery. He would be thought mad at best, and at worst dismissed as the sorriest kind of publicity-seeker. The situation was a profoundly curious one. Mankind had reached the point where people could discuss such things in the abstract and believe in the possibility—even the probability—of nonearthly life. At the same time, if you met a man or heard of a man who claimed that an alien spaceship had landed in his backyard—that was a different proposition. People were not ready for *that*. Royce himself would have dismissed such a story as absurd only a few months ago.

No good could come from blurting out such a yarn. Royce felt that he owed his family something better than that. And he did not try to kid himself. He was what he was; a man can be marked by a strong experience and even changed somewhat, but he does not suddenly become a totally different human being. Royce had his own values, whether they were right or wrong, and they did not include a desire to be a celebrity, a martyr, or a nut to be paraded on television. He wanted a chance to live his own life as best he could, a life that was satisfying and meaningful to him. It was not an outrageous ambition, despite being somewhat unfashionable. Royce believed that perhaps he had earned the right to be himself.

It might be that one day *they* would come again in another place and under other circumstances. If that happened, he was prepared to tell what he knew. It might serve a useful purpose then. It might possibly help to know that *they* were not totally alien, however inexplicable their actions seemed to be. It might help to know that there was a gulf that could be bridged. . . .

Royce did not know and could not guess where the great white sphere had come from, or where it had gone. He did not pretend to understand why the ship had come or what its inhabitants had sought. This small corner of the African earth had been a port of call, a mysterious island touched in the course of an alien Odyssey. Somewhere, perhaps, on a world lost in the deeps of space, there was a Homer who would sing of that voyage, sing of Earth and the beings who lived there.

Royce dared to hope that *they* had learned something good about man. He dared to hope that the songs—if songs there were—might say that men were something more than savages, that they had a capacity for understanding, that there was something in them that could be respected. Yes, and that there was a toughness in man, that they were not to be despised as potential friends in the maelstrom of the universe.

It was only a hope, but it was something.

It could have been worse, for both of them.

Meanwhile, Royce had his own life before him.

It wasn't much, one man's life.

But it always came down to that in the end.

One man. One life.

A DAY CAME when work was done, a time when Royce could take off on his own without guilt and without worry. It was not his last day at the Baboonery but the end was in sight. It was a time of hiatus, a time of waiting, a time for winding up one phase of his life. The new man had not yet arrived but Kathy had started her packing. The kids were playing with furious energy, excited at the prospect of flying away to a distant land called home.

It was a day that had to be.

Royce knew that he would see Buck again this day. He knew that he would have his chance. Call it the sure instinct of the hunter or give it a fancier name, it did not matter. Buck would be waiting.

He took the .375 and the cameras and the glasses. He took one man with him—Mutisya.

They set out together in the battered Land Rover, an unspoken bond between them.

It was a perfect afternoon for hunting: a time of

golden sunlight and soft shadows and cool green leaves. Royce drove slowly, savoring it all, wanting to remember. The Land Rover whined and growled along the weed-grown trail. Through the thick bush where the tsetse flies waited, past the clearing where Matt Donaldson's camp was neat and clean again in anticipation of a fresh covey of hunters from Nairobi. Across the sparkling silver of the Kikumbuliu, once more a gentle stream, and finally out into that great green plain that swept away to the Tsavo. Under that immense African sky, a sky empty now of menace but still a vast sky that went on forever. . . .

Royce saw game that quickened the heart, game that was plentiful with the new grass and water, game that lived as it had lived for uncounted thousands of years. Gray-brown kudu, long-horned oryx, striped zebras that ran in a field of yellow flowers, ungainly ostriches trotting along with the single-minded determination of long-distance runners, dignified old elephants secure in their conviction of immortality. It required a conscious effort of the imagination to realize that the United States, too, had once presented such a picture. The animals had been different, of course, but the scene had been much the same: buffalo and antelope, bears and bobcats, deer and coyotes in an unspoiled land. It took even more of an effort to realize that the days of the old Africa were numbered, that this Pleistocene panorama before his eyes would be gone within fifty years or so.

Royce knew that he was seeing something that would never come again. It was a terrible loss, no matter how inevitable it might be. It left a hole in the world. He wanted to fight it but he recognized that the odds were hopeless. He, too, was an anachronism. He was out of step—or other people were.

He took some pictures. They were not for himself; the only pictures he wanted he carried in his head. The photographs were for the magazine articles he would be writing. A man had to eat.

He did not use his rifle. There was only one animal he wanted now.

He could smell the big river, a cool fresh wetness carried on the rising wind.

He stopped the Land Rover on the rim of the Tsavo valley. He climbed outside, the breeze from the river stirring against his skin. The Tsavo seemed still and quiet in the distance, a river of glass winding across the earth. The flood scars were still plainly visible but there was no fury now. The green meadow sloped peacefully away to the river, alive with new grass and flowers and the rustlings of the wind.

He lifted his binoculars, but it was Mutisya who spotted them first.

"*Kuro*," he said, pointing to his left. "Waterbuck."

Royce nodded. Buck would be there, waiting.

He took the .375 from the cab of the Land Rover. The rifle was cold and heavy in his hands.

The two men moved down into the valley on foot, quartering across the gentle slope. There wasn't much cover—the tall, swaying grass, a few clumps of commiphora—but the wind was right. If they were careful, they should be able to get very close.

Royce was certain that he had him. He had been on too many hunts not to know.

They worked their way down until they were within two hundred yards of the unsuspecting animals. Royce stopped, half hidden in the grass. He stood very still, watching.

There were four of them, all males, standing quietly in the grass near the river. Royce caught their scent clearly—a strong smell, rather like turpentine, but with a heavy animal muskiness. There were four of them, but he saw only one.

Old Buck stood a little apart from the others. He was not a herd animal.

He was a stately creature; he carried himself with aloof dignity, his head up, his splendid horns like a lyre above his alert, rounded ears. He was a majestic animal, a great stag of legend come to claim his world. His sleek coat glowed redly in the westering sun. The white lines that striped his eyes gave him a painted, ceremonial look. The deep curve of his chest told of power that had never known defeat, while the white on his rump hinted at an odd and unexpected playfulness.

Buck must have weighed a quarter of a ton but he stood as delicately balanced as a gazelle.

Royce knelt down and raised his rifle. He got Buck's big chest in the cross hairs of his scope. It was easy, very easy.

He felt nothing, nothing at all.

His finger tightened on the trigger.

Royce made no decision with his conscious mind.

The choice came from deep within him. His rifle moved. Not much, just a little. But enough. There was only a small brown rock in his scope.

He fired.

The flat sound of the shot cracked and echoed in the valley of the Tsavo. A puff of dust and splinters exploded from the rock. The four waterbuck were catapulted into sudden motion. They bolted for the river, Buck in the lead.

They ran without hesitation into the water. The animals were strong, graceful swimmers. They made it across with effortless ease. Royce watched them climb out, dripping, on the far bank.

It was still an easy shot. He held his fire.

The last sight he had of Buck was his white rump—a neat circle like a painted target—vanishing into the high grass.

Mutisya was utterly disgusted.

"Missed him," Royce said, grinning broadly.

Mutisya was not fooled. He felt cheated. "Someone else will kill him, Mr. Royce."

"Not today, anyhow. Maybe he's got a few years left."

Mutisya shook his head. He had no sentimentality about animals. Meat was meat.

Royce felt good about what he had done. There were times when a man had a choice. He had no compulsion to explain his actions even if he could find the words. He thought that he understood a little about himself now; perhaps in time he would understand more. It was not a new thing with him but it was a conviction that had been strengthened by what had happened to him—and by what had not happened. Surely, if man could find a point of contact and identity with beings from another world then there must be a kind of continuity between the creatures that shared the earth. There would be other days when choices could be made. His gesture had been a small one; he was only one imperfect human being. Still, there were articles he could write, pictures he could take, actions that were within his grasp. Perhaps there was a place on this earth where something could be saved. . . .

The two men walked slowly back up the slope to the Land Rover. Mutisya said nothing more, but the burden of his disapproval was heavy. Royce did not doubt that Mutisya would be leading the new man down to the Tsavo for a crack at Buck before long.

Well, maybe the new man would be a lousy shot.

Maybe not.

They climbed into the Land Rover and started back toward the Baboonery. Long before they reached the Kikumbuliu Mutisya spotted some kudu on the grassy plain. He looked a question at Royce.

Royce stopped the Land Rover. He handed the rifle to Mutisya. Mutisya's seamed face creased in an eager smile. He was out of the vehicle in an instant, maneuvering for a clear shot.

Royce watched him and responded to the ancient thrill of the hunt. There was a streak of common clay in him; he could not think of himself as a vegetarian. Man had been a hunter for hundreds of thousands of years before he had sown his first crop. The plants of the field have shallow roots; there are other roots that go deeper.

It was an old drama that was set in its ways and it was soon over: the stalk, the crisp shot, the fall, and death where there had been life.

He helped Mutisya drag the heavy warm body to the road and heave it into the back of the Land Rover. The two men climbed back into the cab and started off again. Mutisya was pleased and happy.

The dead kudu flopped and rolled bonelessly in the back of the vehicle. The soft liquid eyes were dull and glazed, like blobs of old jelly. The dry horns scraped and clicked against metal. There was a lot of thick blood. The big flies covered the animal, feasting.

The great dark shadows were gathering again in the bush. The wind stirred across the lonely land with the first chill of the approaching night.

The dead kudu was very close behind him but Royce tried to force it from his mind. This had been one of the good days. There were other things to remember.

He looked up when he could, out through the dirty windshield, up at that tremendous arch of blue African sky. It was a more mysterious sky to him now, a sky filled with danger and promise, but still a sky that touched the world of man. It was a sky as boundless as it had been when the earth was born.

Life was just beginning, even now.

If he could have a little luck—if he could remember

well enough and long enough—he could carry the memory of that free African sky with him wherever he had to go.

It was a long way home.

Royce hoped that he would not lose it, somewhere along the way.